Goodbye Vietnam

Love, War and Espionage in Vietnam

Dell Isham

DELL ISHAM

outskirtspress
DENVER, COLORADO

Goodbye Vietnam
Love, War and Espionage in Vietnam
All Rights Reserved.
Copyright © 2012 Dell Isham
v2.0

Cover Photo © 2012 JupiterImages Corporation. All rights reserved - used with permission.

Outskirts Press, Inc.
http://www.outskirtspress.com

ISBN: 978-1-4327-9479-8

Library of Congress Control Number: 2012911056

Outskirts Press and the "OP" logo are trademarks belonging to Outskirts Press, Inc.

PRINTED IN THE UNITED STATES OF AMERICA

*This novel is dedicated to my children
-- Shane, Shaun, and Shannon --
who had the fortune and misfortune
of growing up with a combat veteran
and a politician for a father*

One Summer

One summer I bought a kite
I went to the beach to fly it where the sky and the ocean were blue
And the sand and clouds were white
I watched for hours my kite fluttering and hovering in the wind,
But when I wasn't looking
My kite was taken
Out to the ocean, never to be seen again.

by Shaun Isham
9/13/86

CHAPTER 1

"You no love me."

"Open the damn gate!" Captain Clint McGregor yelled at two lethargic Vietnamese soldiers sitting on folding chairs with rifles leaning against them. Clint mumbled to himself, "No wonder we're losing the fucking war." A small shapely Vietnamese girl about 20 years old stood beside him and held his hand tightly.

A corporal sitting in an Army Jeep on the outside of the tall steel gate honked his horn and glared at the guards. The two tired looking Vietnamese soldiers struggled to their feet, appeared to move as slowly as possible and unlatched the gate. They took their time opening it.

Clint imagined the guards quickly glancing at each other with a secret smile.

The Vietnamese are experts in passive resistance, he thought.

The driver swiftly drove into the courtyard, saluted, and jumped out to help the captain with his duffel bags. He piled them in the back seat of the dusty olive-drab Jeep.

"Sorry I'm a little late, sir. Traffic in Can Tho is FUBAR today."

"It's fucked up every day. If you don't die from a wreck, the air pollution will kill you."

Once the captain's gear was stowed, the corporal climbed

back into the drivers' seat of the Jeep.

The Vietnamese girl now held the captain's left hand with both of her hands. With her head bowed and pleading, long straight shiny black hair hung over his arm. He felt sorry for her but he did not know how to calm her.

Speaking quietly so the corporal could not hear him, "Honey, I don't want to go either. But I have to. My country says I must leave Vietnam." He gently raised her head with his right hand under her chin. Her face was streaked with tears and sweat and mucus. Her eyes were dark and sunken because she had not slept in three days. He still saw her as beautiful. He leaned down to kiss her swollen trembling lips but she turned her head.

"You no love me," she blubbered in her broken English, which Clint always found endearing. She could always get her point of view across whether she had the right words or not.

"Lien, I stayed as long as I could. They won't let me stay any longer. I have to go. Please don't be this way."

"You number ten soldier."

"No Lien. I'm not a bad person. I've been number one to you."

"You go America. I no go. Now no Vietnamee like me. Maybe I be dead. How you like? I love you. You no love me back. You go to wife. You boom-boom. Maybe you have *beaucoup* keeds. Maybe your American wife no love you."

The captain was starting to get embarrassed. Tears came to his eyes too. "Lien, please don't do this. I'll write you letters. I'll try to come back." He attempted to hold her shaking body close but she pushed away.

"When you boom-boom wife, you think of me?"

"Yes, Lien. Yes."

"You lie. You always lie. Me no good wife to you?"

"Captain, we're ready to go now," the corporal said pretending to be oblivious to the domestic spat. "There's still room in the back seat."

"No, I'll sit up front," even though officers were expected to sit in the back, not in front with an enlisted man. Clint hated the class distinctions in the Army. He disregarded the social norms of the military whenever possible.

They were just about through the gate when Clint yelled, "Stop!" He realized he had not answered Lien's last question. He did not want to leave her that way.

He jumped out of the Jeep and ran back to her. She appeared to be in a state of shock, her big brown eyes focused on nothing. Clint tried to put his arms around her but she pushed away. So, he grabbed her arm. "Lien," he said a little sternly, "look at me. You're a wonderful wife, wonderful lover; there will always be a place in my heart for you. I promise."

He felt guilty as hell. *Maybe I ruined her life for selfish purposes — for a home life, for companionship, for sex . . .*

"You lie. You go. I die now." She pulled away from him and ran toward the apartment building where they shared a room. Then she stopped, turned around, and stood alone.

Clint jumped back in the Jeep and turned to look at her. He saw a miserable young woman in light colored pajamas wearing cheap flip-flops. Strands of black hair plastered her face. She stood with her arms stiffly at her side, tiny fists clenched, face swollen, staring at him.

Surely she must have known this day was coming. We did not talk about it because I didn't know how to explain this to her and she didn't want to hear about me leaving. She must know we can't control our lives in a war zone. I'd love to spend the rest of my life with her but she couldn't adjust to American society. Or am I just rationalizing? She had said she would rather be American than Vietnamese, but she wouldn't be happy in the United States.

Clint managed a small smile and a subdued wave. Lien did not respond. She just stared. She was less than five-feet tall and got smaller and smaller as the Jeep left the courtyard and passed the two guards. He kept looking back and she kept staring. He knew this image of her would be seared into his brain forever.

After driving four blocks in dense traffic the corporal tried to make conversation. "Looking forward to getting home, sir?"

"Yes I am." And then added absent mindedly, ". . . but it's hard to leave someone after you've lived with them for a year." The driver nodded. Then Clint remembered there would be no one to meet him when his plane landed in Oakland the next morning. His wife was staying with her parents in Wyoming and she wrote him to say there was no reason to make an expensive trip to California just to meet him.

Clint was absorbed in thought. The driver and Clint did not say another word to each other all the way to the airport. Clint did not see the market where he tried out his Vietnamese language skills buying food. He did not see the pharmacy where one could buy any type of antibiotic, Chinese herb, and different kinds of ground animal horn to improve sex. He did not see the families camped outside the hospital because they had a sick or injured relative inside. He did not see the smiling old women with red gums and black teeth from constantly chewing betel nut to relieve pain. He was not aware of the loud rapping noise of thousands of motor scooters, or the smell of sewage, or the sight of garbage piled in the street median.

They drove past the office of the Chinese doctor where Lien got her illegal abortion. It cost 400 American dollars. It was the day Lien came home and pulled a pile of tissue out from her purse and opened it to reveal a smear of blood.

"Oh, it gone now. You-me babysaun," she said with some pride in her voice. "You-me make."

He could not understand her reaction. He was disgusted and remorseful.

She was tired all the time after that operation so she went to the doctor on a regular basis to get Vitamin B-12 shots.

When the corporal and captain arrived at the airport Clint did not notice the inlaid colored tiles decorating the building and the sidewalk which were once beautiful, but now dirty and covered with concertina wire. He did not see the bullet holes in the airport terminal that were a reminder of the Tet Offensive of 1968.

Lien had told him the Viet Cong had killed and injured so many people the South Vietnamese officials were overwhelmed. They dug huge pits and used bulldozer to push the bodies of the dead, injured, and crying babies into the holes and covered them with dirt. She had tears in her eyes when she remembered this.

It did not take long to board the Tiger Airlines airplane with the large friendly stewardesses who handed out pillows, patted the soldiers on the shoulder and thanked them for serving their country. He had expected a celebration from the passengers because they had survived and were heading home, but it was quiet, very very quiet.

Clint imagined his fellow passenger saw no reason to celebrate because they were thinking about what they had seen and what they had done. Many would be ashamed the rest of their lives, he thought, and would tell no one but they could not get rid of the memories. Some would be plagued by nightmares and panic attacks. Others may become alcoholics and beat their wives. Some would commit suicide. Others, he knew, could block what happened so completely they would not think about it again until they were on their deathbed fifty years later and maybe ask God for forgiveness.

In reality, he also knew that many never saw the enemy close-up and would not be traumatized by their experience.

Some left lovers and children behind, hoping the Communists would not punish them.

When it became dark he allowed tears to come to his eyes and he grieved. *What have I done to you, Lien?*

CHAPTER 2
"So much for solitude."

"Mr. McGregor, as you know, this meeting is your annual review. You've been teaching at our high school for ten years and I thought we better meet personally," the gaunt school superintendent said without making eye contact.

"You've got my full attention," Clint McGregor said, not liking the body language on display across the large desk from him.

"I know you had an impressive military career, have lived many places in the world, and have good experience to impart. And the students like your classes. You're popular with the students."

Compliments are often the prelude to criticism, Clint assumed. "They just like my war stores. Actually, I worked for the CIA when I was in the Army."

"That's not in your record."

"And it better stay that way," Clint said with a smirk. "If I told you more, I'd have to kill you."

The superintendent looked Clint in the eye for the first time to see if he was kidding.

Clint enjoyed making his boss feel uncomfortable and did not change his facial expression.

The superintendent gulped. "Are you taking this review seriously?"

"Very."

"And you got a Bronze Star in Vietnam? What was that for?"

"Oh, that's just a 'Good Conduct Metal' for officers."

"I see. Very well, let's get started." The superintendent then looked at his expensive watch.

Clint figured the gesture was to show him how busy and important he was. Clint crossed his legs and leaned back in his chair to indicate he was not impressed.

"Teachers are accountable these days. Whether you are popular or not with the students doesn't matter. What matters to the school board and the public is how well your students do on the standardized exams. To be frank, your students are doing poorly."

"That's because the tests are doing poorly, not because the students or the teacher are doing poorly."

"That's irrelevant," the superintendent said with a little hoarseness creeping into his voice.

"I don't teach to the tests. I teach to their future lives. I teach them to read and write and think for themselves. I teach them how to make decisions. I teach them how to resolve conflicts. I teach them to cope and achieve in a world that does not yet exist."

"That all sounds very idealistic. But you're a history teacher, not a philosopher."

"I'm giving you my philosophy of teaching history."

"And I don't believe you have been filing your goals and objectives. At least you have not submitted any to your principal."

"That's because I don't have any. I respond to individual needs."

"And that's why your students are doing poorly on the standardized tests. It's the scores on those tests that determine your rating, the school's rating, and my rating. It also influences our school funding and we can't afford low test scores."

"You and I know it's all bullshit," Clint said in a calm but assertive manner.

The superintendent took a deep breath, and said, "We don't have room here for revolutionaries."

"I come from a long line of revolutionaries. I had scores of ancestors killed in the American Revolution. I had relatives injured registering black folks to vote during the Civil Rights Movement. I had a cousin knocked silly by the pigs at the Chicago Democratic National Convention in 1968. He's never been the same since."

"Again, interesting, but irrelevant. Maybe you're just too old to learn new tricks. We could hire two 24-year-old teachers for what we're paying you. You're 60. You could take retirement now if you want."

"Please put that in writing so I can sue your ass."

"There's no need for that kind of language here." The school superintendent looked a little shaken when he stood and said, "We'll be announcing your retirement toward the end of the school year. Good luck, Mr. McGregor."

The decision was not a surprise to Clint. He had prepared for this day for some time.

Fortunately his full background never caught up with him. As a young man, after serving in Vietnam, he came home to be elected to the state senate. He never completed his first four-year term, however, explaining that he had business to contend with overseas. That is when he became "Quent Gregory," a soldier-of-fortune who discovered and sold historic artifacts, teamed up with the sexy and intelligent Anita Hampton, and cheated a partner out of most of his share. After a couple years Anita ran off with most of his money. Only two people knew Clint McGregor and Quent Gregory was the same person, his partners in crime. They both had good reason to keep his identify secret, their complicity.

Clint left the school building after his meeting with the school superintendent even though he was required to stay until 4:00 p.m. "What are they going to do, fire me," he grumbled to himself.

I'm being put out to pasture. Before the end of the school year they'll have one of those stupid cake-and-coffee receptions in the teachers' lounge. I'll attend and say how much I'll miss my colleagues and students but it's time to retire.

He was thinking of drinking something stronger than coffee. When he got home he filled a water glass with ice and poured Grey Goose to the brim. *Screw that brain dead superintendent and his minions; I have some plans of my own.*

As Clint had aged he gradually became less and less tolerant of those dumber than him, which as nearly everyone. He had bought a piece of private property near Mountain Rest, South Carolina, surrounded by the Sumter National Forest. Every weekend he worked on building his energy efficient cabin in the woods. For the first time in his life he would be alone, and he was looking forward to it.

Well, not quite true. He had his devoted companion, Lady, a golden retriever, with big soulful brown eyes, a pleasant disposition and shiny reddish blond hair.

Clint figured he could live fine on a teachers' pension, and in a couple years Social Security, in the near self-sufficiency he planned for himself. A creek where he could go fishing was only 50 yards from his back door. He already had his vegetable garden planted. Any deer that walked by his property was liable to get shot for meat.

In his cabin he would be surrounded by books and guns. Outside the cabin he would be surrounded by trees and solitude.

I'm done with intrigue and deception. I'm done with political correctness, phony standards, and the human rat race in general. From now on I'm living for reading, relaxing, and appreciating nature.

There would not be much excitement in his new life but he had already experienced enough excitement for several men. He felt safe, only having to worry about bears, snakes, and an occasional skunk. It was 16 miles of dirt road that ended at his cabin. Solitude is hard to find in South Carolina but he found some. He did not expect any visitors and did not want any.

After the school year concluded he moved to the cabin and did not leave a forwarding address. He soon developed a routine. The morning was reserved for chopping firewood and other chores. In the afternoon he settles in with a good book or listens to National Public Radio with a beer in his hand and Lady by his side.

He never bothered getting a hunting license. He heard deer were over-populating the state, so he was really providing a public service to cull those that came too near his cabin.

After about three months he began to run low on ammunition, reading material and beer. It was time to drive to the nearest highway crossroads. It was inevitable; he was going to have to deal with the asshole at the country store. It was the best place for miles around to buy cheap beer and paperback books. He made the mistake once of telling the store owner he had been a history teacher.

As soon as he entered the little store that advertised fishing worms and boiled peanuts on the same sign, it started all over again.

"Hey, it's the professor. Welcome to my little store. I hope it's OK for y'all, city boy."

Clint mumbled, "It's just fine."

"What'd ya say?"

"It's fine, Floyd."

"It's not like ya got much choice 'round here," he said with a laugh.

"Yeah," Clint said, standing in front of the newspaper stand.

"Hey, if you're gonna read that paper, ya got to buy it."

"Put it on my tab."

"Since you're so smart 'bout history, who was called the 'greatest living soldier in American history?'"

"Knowing you, I'd have to say that would be Robert E. Lee," Clint said, attempting to sound bored.

"Yeah, and you know what? They done took his U.S. citizenship away from him and it weren't restored 'till 1975, more'n a hundred years after he died. What an insult."

Clint just could not help himself: "Lee was damn lucky. Traitors ought to be shot."

He got the reaction he expected.

"You're the one that's a damn traitor. I'm goin' tell Leroy not to sell you no more ammo," Floyd said as he stomped around the store.

"Your great general also surrendered to General Grant at Appomattox Courthouse on April 9, 1865," Clint said, just to rub it in a little more.

"Here's another one professor. Listen up everyone." There were just two other people in the store. "Who were the two inventors in North Carolina who changed the future of transportation?"

"That's an easy one, Floyd. You're slippin.' It was Wilbur and Orville Wright."

"OK, now it's time to play Stump the Professor. Which one of them two boy's lived the longest?"

Clint thought about that for a minute. He knew he had a fifty percent chance of being right but if he guessed the wrong one he would never here the end of it.

"Come on, Mr. Educated City Boy. Maybe my seven years of grade school made me smarter than your seven years of college. It's time for the answer."

"OK, Floyd. You got me there."

"The college educated professor loses again!" he shouted. "It was Orville. He lived 'til 1948, while his brother lived only nine more years after that first flight."

One person back by the coolers applauded and Floyd enjoyed a big belly laugh. Clint, leafing through a magazine, was hoping Floyd would dislocate his shoulder trying to pat himself on the back.

Clint packed his SUV with cases of beer, paperback best sellers, and TV dinners. He paid the gloating Floyd in cash.

His next stop was Leroy's to buy some ammunition. He knew Leroy might agree with Floyd's version of the Civil War but dollars were more important to him than history.

The next afternoon, while sipping a beer on his back deck, Clint heard a chainsaw. *What the hell?* Then he heard a truck engine. *So much for solitude. Can't we leave someplace on Earth for the wild animals, like me?*

Clint tethered Lady, then climbed and slid down the mountain slope in the direction of the unwelcome noise of civilization. From behind a tree, he saw some road building equipment. *Shit.* He thought about sabotaging their machinery when they left, but that would bring even more people into his domain.

The truck, trailer, and Cat all said "Hampton Construction" on the said.

Hampton? Like Anita's last name. She ran off with fortune. Maybe I'm looking at some of it right now.

After the construction crew got their Cat and mobile office unloaded, he heard a female voice yell, "OK boys. That's enough for today. Let's head on back to Pickens and grab some chow."

Then he saw her. It certainly was not Anita. Red hair sticking out from under her hard hat, she stood about five-foot-two, and just as wide. Then he saw her spit tobacco juice about ten yards in front of her. Definitely not Anita.

Clint waited for them to leave, and then he scrambled down to the base camp. Inside the unlocked temporary office he found the specifications for their work. After looking at blueprints for some time he figured their road building would miss his place by 500 yards and they would set up a logging operation on top of the next mountain. It did not look like the road construction was going to bother him much but he would be able to see the clear-cutting on the next ridge.

He jotted down some notes on a scrap of paper and headed back to his mountain retreat after checking out their equipment. From now on he would follow Forest Service timber sale announcements in an attempt to prevent any further destruction of his little piece of the environment.

When he returned to his cabin he felt like he had done a day's work. He looked at his watch: 4:15 p.m. In his world it was 'Happy Hour.' He opened the fridge, grabbed a can of beer, and popped the top, making that familiar snap and fizz sound. Back to his chair on his deck, he put his feet up on the wooden railing.

A few minutes later he drifted back to Vietnam. He saw himself in military garb, smiling, and carrying an M-79 grenade launcher. It was hot, humid and risky. He saw Lien, not quite five feet tall with her long dark hair, wearing a pink flowered tight fitting blouse and loose black satin pajama-style pants. Her delicate hands held a multi-colored umbrella to keep the sun from making her smooth almond skin any darker. Her brown eyes were big, as well as her smile.

"*Lien? Is that you? Ba co khoe khong (How are you)?*"

CHAPTER 3

"Women always want more attention"

<u>Mountain Rest, South Carolina, USA, 2004</u>

Clint sat on the deck of his new cabin, hands behind his head. One disturbing fact of retirement, he thought, it gives one time to contemplate the meaning of their life. Clint remembered the decisions that seemed small at the time but had major unintended consequences. He also remembered the important decisions that were made too casually.

His wife of 25 years threatened to leave him a few years ago and his response was, "Goodbye." Lien, the only real love of his life, begged him to stay or take her with him, but he left Vietnam without her. After a year in Vietnam, the Central Intelligence Agency offered to hire him at three times the salary of an Army captain, but he turned it down. He campaigned for nearly four years to get elected to the state senate, but once winning the office, he did not complete his first term. His life seemed like a series of missed opportunities.

The great adventure of his life was finding valuable historic artifacts, which he had to hide to keep his wealth from those who would take it. And the one he trusted most took it anyway.

He reached down and petted Lady, his golden retriever. Whenever he stopped she pushed her wet nose under his hand to let him know she wanted more attention. *Women always want more attention than it is possible to give*, he thought.

He looked down at her. "Lady, there must be more to life than sitting in the sun, reading a book and drinking beer."

She looked up at him with her big brown eyes and with an understanding look on her face.

"Dogs are a lot smarter than we humans give them credit for."

She responded with a big dog-smile and licked his hand.

"I could do other things. I could take up bird watching, for example. But I don't seem to have the motivation. If those birds want to be counted they're going to have to come to me."

Lady cocked her head and panted as if to say, *No problem. You've got me to watch.*

"We found a nice place to retire, didn't we, Lady?

She perked her ears up and made a low growl.

"I know. The chainsaws. They make me upset too. That hillside over there is stripped bare now. Anything that ever lived there was either mowed down or run off. Remember the day we saw the deer and the elk and the small critters run by our house to flee those destructive humans? And the creek turned muddy, smothering the little fish."

Clint felt silly carrying on a conversation with a dog. But Lady appeared to look interested and did not interrupt. "The timber company says trees would be planted back."

He knew that may be true but not until bulldozers piled up slash, set it on fire, and tree planters stomped all over the ground. Herbicides would be sprayed to keep out unwanted vegetation. Many of the seedlings would survive but all the trees would be the same species, the same age, the same height, and susceptible to the same diseases.

"What's left won't be decent habitat for all the plants and animals that once lived on that hill."

Lady looked up at Clint, trying hard to understand, he thought. She got a sad look on her face because Clint had a sad look on his face.

When he looked down at her he had to laugh. "Cheer-up, old dog. Here, fetch."

He picked up a stick from the deck and threw it into the woods. She bounded from the deck, tail wagging, to do what retrievers are supposed to do, retrieve. She quickly returned to the deck, spirits revived, and dropped the stick at Clint's feet. He chucked her under the chin and praised the delighted animal.

As the sun began to set behind the stripped hillside he opened another beer. When the mosquitoes began to rule the air, Clint knew it was time to go inside.

He looked at the clock, popped a TV dinner into the microwave oven, and estimated he could finish reading John Grisham's latest novel by 11:00 p.m., just in time for bed.

What's on the schedule for tomorrow? What schedule? I'm retired. Nothing much was planned. Maybe another case of beer and another good book to read.

By 11:15 he was sound asleep. His protective animal friend slept at the foot of his bed.

At about 3:00 in the morning Clint awoke with a tremendous jolt. He could not catch his breath. He felt his heart pounding. He sat up quickly and after a few minutes his breathing and heartbeat returned to normal. Instantly he thought he knew why he had awakened.

Had Lien died? In the middle of the night such thoughts

seem so real. A tear trickled down the right side of his face.

He remembered how she took care of him in a war zone and kept him sane while so many others were losing touch with reality. Lien was Clint's loving companion in Vietnam for a year and asked for nothing in return except kindness.

He remembered the letter she wrote him just before the communists took over. She sent a snapshot of herself with her pudgy little son from a previous relationship. At the time both Lien and Clint expected it would be their last communication.

Then one day in 1977, she called on the phone and asked for, "Senator Crint." He smiled at the thought of the unexpected event. On her own she had made it half way around the world to Salem, Oregon.

He remembered her telling him how she suffered to escape on a sinking fishing boat, crashed on a deserted island, and was put into an Indonesian refugee camp for a year.

"I failed her," he mumbled in the darkened room. *She finally made it to America two years after the communists took over. She suffered because of me. Those who befriended Americans were persecuted. They were sent to reeducation camps, drafted into the military, or stripped of their land or profession. Those who escaped, or tried to, experienced tremendous hardship.*

Lady was now awake and putting her nose on top of the sheet near Clint's head. He patted her.

Clint settled back into his pillow and mourned the opportunity he had lost, not spending his life with Lien. *My wife left because she said she was tired of my Vietnam nightmares. I probably said Lien's name in my sleep one too many times.*

He did not go back to sleep. Instead, he tried to relive the year they were together when she came to Oregon.

Clint remembered she called and said, "Come see me. I be at Catholic Charities." He could not believe it. They went to dinner that night and spent as much time together as possible for the next year.

She was very jealous. She wanted Clint to leave his family for her. He could not blame her for feeling that way but she refused to understand that he had other responsibilities too – a family, the legislature, his real estate business. She wanted all his time. That would have been wonderful but impossible.

Clint knew he would eventually lose her. And he did. He knew he would always live with regret afterwards.

He begged her to stay.

After learning proper English, getting the equivalent of a high school education and passing college entrance exams, she said she wanted to go to college in the Northeast where she had relatives. She said she would come back to her 'Crint' someday.

When she left she said, "Crint, you have good life now. I am your mistress. I love you but I want a good life too and I want a good life for Vinh. I can give him a good life by being a good example."

Clint was used to debating every day in the legislature, but his powers of persuasion failed him. "Lien, you can go to school here if you want to. If you want to be independent of my financial support you can be. You don't have to leave me to be independent. Please stay. I love you."

"Crint, I love you too. But as long as I am with you I will be dependent upon you. It is too easy. I am 27 years old now. If I am going to go to school I need to go now. We can write to each other. If you love me you will let me go to find my life. I do not want to leave you but you are not here for me. I need one-woman man; do not you see? Maybe I will not like it; maybe I will be back. You should wish me well. I wish you have a happy life. I am not happy much of the time because I am jealous; I know that. It torments me – that's a new word for me – torment. You torment me. It is not fair to me; do not you see?"

Clint got out of bed, stretched, patted Lady on the head again, and said, "That bad dream sure set off a lot of memories."

Getting a cup of coffee, he decided he would email Lien to make sure she was all right. It was just a nightmare after all.

He stepped out on the deck, coffee in hand, and sat down on the blue Adirondack chair. It was already getting warm outside. *A shot of whiskey and a dollop of whipped cream on top would sure go good with this strong hot coffee. Living with a constant .02 blood alcohol content is a good way to go.*

CHAPTER 4
Standing in Line

In the isolation of his cabin in the woods Clint thought about his year in South Vietnam. He did not know whether he should smile or frown. His memories of the place were still clear in his mind even though it was only a year out of a lifetime. That experience changed him but he could never decide whether it was for the better.

In the 30-day leave before going overseas he visited his parents in Salem, Oregon. One day he and his father toured the State Capitol. When they got to the senate gallery they looked down from the balcony to see the senate floor. The legislature was not in session so the dignified cavernous room was empty, quiet and dimly lit.

"I'd like sit down there someday," Clint quietly told his father.

"I don't see why not."

"Maybe I'll run for the legislature when I get back." _If I get back?_ was unspoken.

After returning to his parent's house he began packing. The feeling of apprehension returned. Clint did not know what to expect but he had seen the fire fights and body bags on television. The unknown was disconcerting.

With his leave ended he flew to San Francisco and stood in line to board a military bus to Oakland. There was a lot of standing in line when he arrived in Oakland too.

Standing in a line is a big part of the military, particularly in training. Clint vowed, once out of the Army, he would never stand in line again.

He remembered with a smile that as a cadet he once told a drill sergeant, "If you die before I do, I won't be pissing on your grave."

The sergeant was ignorant enough to ask, "Why's that?"

"Because I hate standing in line."

That comment cost him 50 push-ups but it was worth it.

Soldiers of all ranks and grades began moving forward to board a plane with "Tiger Airlines" painted on the side.

"I never heard of Tiger Airlines," he said to no one in particular.

A soldier in line ahead of him said in a low voice, "It's operated by the CIA."

Clint thought this piece of information, or misinformation, was interesting but not reassuring as to the safety of the airline. *It's not like I have a choice of airlines,* he thought.

A passenger on the plane boasted, "This is my second tour of duty in 'Nam."

"Hell, that's nothin,' I'm goin' fer the third time. Can't get enough of those Vietnamese dames," another soldier boasted.

The first timers, who were the great majority, pretended to be confident.

Clint wondered how many on the plane would return in a box. He knew the lifespan of a lieutenant in combat was quite short.

"You company grade officers last 'bout two months in a combat zone," one grizzled sergeant laughed upon seeing Clint's insignia.

Clint chuckled nervously in response.

As the flight took off, he felt fortunate to have a row of three seats by himself in order to stretch out but it also made him feel isolated. As the plane droned on for hours he read a news magazine from cover to cover and wondered if any of the articles were of any importance to him since he might not live much longer.

The flight across the Pacific was long and boring. He dozed uncomfortably and when he awoke all he saw outside the window was ocean. Flying halfway around the world was a lesson in comprehending the size of planet Earth. It made Clint wonder why the U.S. even cared what happened so far from home.

Clint convinced himself that he was taking part in a historically important event. He knew the odds were that he would return alive and if he did not go to Vietnam the next generation would be asking why he did not go.

The pilot interrupted his slumber with an announcement over the address system. "If you will look out the right side of the aircraft you'll see the Island of Saipan; the site of an important battle in World War II."

He looked at the small island below. It was dominated by an airfield and a couple buildings that looked like hotels.

For Clint, the irony was great. He remembered his father saying he was stationed in Saipan. Thousands were killed fighting over this speck in the middle of the Pacific. Now he was passing over it on his way to fight in the next generation's war.

When he had asked his father what he did in World War II, the response was that he played a lot of softball. When pressed, his father would relent and say it was his job to deliver toilet paper to the troops.

The next morning Lieutenant Clint McGregor saw Vietnam for the first time. Shades of green and blue merged; from the air it looked peaceful, tranquil and beautiful. As the plane descended he saw the bomb craters and vegetation stripped away from the roadsides. He learned later that cleared highway shoulders discouraged ambushes and the mining of the road.

As he stepped off the plane he poked his head into a blast furnace. The hundred degree temperature was a shock after spending hours in the air conditioned airplane.

As he walked down the steps to the tarmac Clint saw many Vietnamese workers in what appeared to be black uniforms scurrying about. At first he thought they were Viet Cong but quickly learned the black pajama was the common dress of the peasant.

The airport terminal was small for the declared "busiest airport in the world." It was no refuge from the oppressive heat. People were all jammed together, most yelling in a language he did not understand.

He found a men's restroom and splashed grayish water on his hands, face and arms. The water, which was not exactly cool, felt good on the back of his neck. Inside a stall he noticed there was no toilet paper, just squares of newspaper stuck on a nail protruding from the wall. Also on the wall someone had written in English, "The only thing I feel when I shoot a Gook is the recoil of my rifle."

His group was soon hustled over to an open air building

with a corrugated metal roof, where of course, they were told to stand in line. Soon everyone passed by a long table with enlisted men standing behind piles of olive drab uniforms. They yelled, "What's your size? What's your size?"

Instantly a duffel bag, shirts, pants, socks and a slouchy hat rained down on each of the men in line.

Then it was get-in-another-line in the hot sun waiting for transportation. Sweltering buses hauled them to another line to process paperwork and schedule assignments.

When Clint finally got to the head of this line an enlisted man intently looked at a roster and asked, "What're you doing here? You're supposed to be in North Carolina at language school."

"Well, I'm here now and here are my new orders," Clint said, handing the clerk a copy of his printed orders. "But if you want to send me back, that's OK with me."

"Stand over there until I figure out what to do with you. I'll call you."

Clint, with sweat dripping into his eyes, walked with his heavy duffel bag to the designated spot in the shade and leaned against a concrete wall.

His name was not called for a long time. *Maybe I'll just spend my year in Vietnam leaning against this wall.*

After what seemed like hours Clint found the need for a restroom again.

Bathroom philosophers were busy at this location too. On the wall someone had written, "Never has so much been fucked up for so many by so few."

After waiting for hours in the heat Clint finally heard his name called.

"Lieutenant McGregor . . . Lieutenant McGregor . . . Ho, there you are. I thought maybe the VC got you, sir. OK, OK, I think I've got this straightened out. Your original orders were changed."

"Yes, that's why I gave you a copy of my new orders, corporal," Clint said, somewhat perturbed and feeling as though he was dying of thirst.

"Well, you've been assigned to be a Phoenix Advisor and you're going to Sa Dec Province."

"What's a Phoenix Advisor?"

"I have absolutely no idea, sir. Somebody will eventually tell ya."

"Where is Sa Dec Province?"

"Somewhere in South Vietnam."

"Thanks, that's a great help."

"Hey, I'm just a clerk. They only tell me how to process the paperwork."

"OK. How am I going to get there?"

"Well, you're sure as hell ain't goin' to drive there unless you want to get your ass shot off. You're scheduled to go on a helicopter," the clerk said looking down at his papers. "It looks like it's three days from now."

"Three days? What am I supposed to do in the meantime?"

"Well, sir," he pointed. "You see that barracks over there?"

"Yeah."

"That's where you're going to wait. Step down the line and pick up some sheets and a pillow. You won't need any blankets," the clerk laughed. "Welcome to South Vietnam . . . Next."

Clint picked up his sheets and pillow as directed and walked to the barracks that was about 50 yards away. The loneliness he felt on the airplane was compounded.

The barracks was big but he noticed that only a few of the bunks had sheets on them.

"I don't know a soul on this whole continent. I don't know what my job is. And I don't even know where I'm going," he mumbled.

First he found a drinking fountain. Then he took his time making up his metal framed bed. Upon completing this little task and emptying his duffel bag, he realized he was the only occupant in his row of bunks. A line of lockers running the length of the barracks isolated him from any of the other rows.

The rest of the afternoon he lay on his bunk reading the paperback book he brought. The title of the book was <u>The Boss</u>, about Chicago Mayor Richard Daily. He clearly remembered the riot at the 1968 Democratic Convention in Chicago where police battered and bloodied protesters, including one of his relatives, with the support of Mayor Daily. It was the confrontation that helped Richard Nixon narrowly defeat Senator Hubert Humphrey for president. *Now Nixon is my commander-in-chief.*

That night he heard a couple soldiers from a few rows away talking loudly enough to be heard. His ears perked up when he heard one of them say, "Yeah, I'm a Phoenix Advisor and I'm glad as hell to be getting the hell out of here."

"How was it? I mean being out there in the swamps," the other soldier asked in a falsely nonchalant manner.

"Well, I made it out alive, didn't I? That means it was all right. See this here scar right here. That's where I almost didn't make it. But you ought to see the other guy. Fucker. The worms are eatin' him right now.

They both laughed.

"Well, I guess you did all right then, huh?"

"I saw too many people get killed. Never forget something like that, particularly when they're standin' right next to ya when they get it. Come to think of it, yeah, I did OK. But I'm not countin' my chickens yet. The Viet Cong just might raid this place tonight and kill us all."

"Are you serious?"

"Fuck no. They can't get us here. Even the VC don't like suicide missions. It's only them dumb ass monks that set themselves on fire. Talk about crazy . . . Much better to get a bullet in the head. Quit askin' so many fuckin' questions, man; I got to get some beauty rest. I'm outa here tomorrow at 0600 hours. You can have this God forsaken place; I'm leavin.'"

Clint thought, *In that little exchange I didn't learn much about being a Phoenix Advisor except that they get shot at. Maybe I'm that guy's replacement. This sounds like some serious stuff. Oh well, I wonder where the mess hall is. I'm getting hungry but I'm sure not going to wander around in the dark looking for it. I'll just follow the others in the morning to the food."*

And the next morning that is exactly what he did. It was a Navy mess hall with an abundance and variety of foods to choose from the buffet line. Clint selected steak, scrambled eggs, toast, orange juice and coffee. Everything tasted good and fresh except the coffee. The coffee tasted like it had been strained through a brown paper hand towel. Knowing he had time to kill he ate slowly.

Then it was back to the barracks to read his book. He wondered what he would do after finishing reading the biography of Mayor Daily. He also wondered how he would get to the helicopter to transport himself to Sa Dec.

The next day he was called to the supply room where he was issued a M16 rifle, ammo with two magazines, and a flack jacket. Both the rifle and the jacket looked well worn. The jacket was heavy and smelled of body odor. The rifle needed cleaning. He took the weapon apart, cleaned it, and put it back together several times just for practice.

Clint chastised himself for feeling bored as he waited for his flight; at least he was not getting shot at and he should be grateful for that. Time dragged so slowly that he found himself spending as much time as possible in the mess hall talking to strangers. He walked a couple blocks in every direction from the large barracks. He would have liked to become a tourist but was not sure where he could go, and not being able to estimate the danger, he stayed on the base. One afternoon Clint was assigned to take a class on Vietnamese etiquette and geography. Getting more familiar with the Vietnamese culture was something he would welcome once he was transported to his assignment.

At the class he picked up a map of Vietnam and took it back to his bunk. He studied the map for some time before he found the name, "Sa Dec." The place looked to be right in the middle of the Mekong Delta, and surrounded by water. Sa Dec was the name of a city as well as the name for the province. He saw that his helicopter ride would take him southeast of Saigon.

On the third day, shortly after breakfast, a sergeant came to the barracks yelling, "Lieutenant McGregor! Is there a Lieutenant McGregor here?"

"Over here."

"Grab yer gear and follow me, sir. Leave the sheets and pillow right there. You won't be needin' 'em. Put on yer flack jacket. We're gettin' you outa here. Bring everythin' else with ya."

Clint followed the fast strutting sergeant for a quarter mile around concrete and temporary buildings until they came to a clearing where a helicopter was idling on the ground, swirling dust in every direction.

"There ya are," the sergeant said, motioning toward the dust storm. "Good luck," the sergeant said. The sarge stayed behind while Clint ducked, squinted his eyes, and scurried toward the 'copter.

He hefted his duffel bag toward the open side of the aircraft and the gunner grabbed it and threw it toward the back of the helicopter.

It was the first time Clint had ridden in a helicopter, so he was not quite sure how to board the craft. He stood on the landing struts and with difficulty boosted himself into the doorway. It was a doorway without doors he soon realized.

The pilot turned and nodded to him and the co-pilot looked at the cockpit gauges. The gunner yelled something he could not hear over the noise of the aircraft. Clint sat on a canvas seat and fumbled with a safety belt. He noticed no one else was wearing a seat belt, so he gave up on the idea. Suddenly his stomach dropped as the helicopter lifted off the ground and took a long nearly sideways angle to the south. It reminded him of the thrill of a carnival ride except more dangerous.

Shortly after they lifted off Clint saw a residential area of Saigon made from scrap plywood and cardboard, corrugated metal, olive drab canvas, yellow and blue plastic tarps, and flattened tin cans. The streets were dusty except for piles of garbage. Soon he saw scarred hillsides, rice patties, and then gray defoliated jungle with sickly looking dirty brown streams. The further they went the more bomb craters he saw. Because of the prop noise no communication was possible, so Clint just stared out the open doorway and watched the scenery. As they traveled south the landscape turned to natural shades of green and waterways were visible as they reflected the sun.

That was over 40 years ago, Clint thought. *It was the beginning of my adventure in Vietnam.*

He stretched and walked to the kitchen to get another beer.

CHAPTER 5

"Workin' for the CIA"

Lap Vo, South Vietnam, 1970

Twenty minutes later the co-pilot of the helicopter reached back and waved to get Clint's attention and then pointed to a large ramshackle dark wooden building below.

They circled the barb wire surrounded compound twice before setting down on a concrete chopper pad. The gunner took Clint's duffel bag and threw it to the ground.

This time Clint could hear the pilot loud and clear. He yelled, "Get out! Get out!"

Clint climbed out of the 'copter. As his feet hit the ground the helicopter quickly ascended into the sky. He stood there alone for a few seconds wondering what to do next. Just then an enlisted man ran out of the building with "Team House" written on the side with white paint.

"Good morning, sir. I'm PFC James. I'll show you to your quarters and introduce you around," he said as he picked up the duffel bag and hefted it over one shoulder.

Clint started to raise his right arm, ready to return a salute, but there was none to return.

Private James looked at him and said, "We don't salute around here. This way, sir."

When they got to the team house, just 40 meters from the landing pad, he met six other enlisted men and officers and one civilian. He was greeted in a nonchalant manner by men in non-regulation uniforms and most wearing sandals instead of canvas combat boots. He was told to pick any vacant room he wanted as his bedroom.

Clint expected to report to a commanding officer, which was normal military protocol when coming to a new assignment, but no one stepped forward.

As Clint stood making up his bed and setting mosquito netting in the large room he had selected for himself, the civilian with a slight build and wearing a polo shirt and tan slacks, came into his room.

"How's it going? If you have any questions as you get used to your new assignment, please don't hesitate to ask me or anyone else," he said. "Anything you need? Do not drink the water, do not walk to the village alone, and if you have to drive into Sa Dec in our Jeep for any reason, wait until a couple hours after sunrise. Most of the roadside bombs will have been detonated by then. This village is called 'Lap Vo,' but you know that."

Stepping forward as if to share a secret the civilian continued, "This is considered to be a 'pacified' area but that does not mean there are no snipers or land mines. There is a curfew around here. It is 2200 hours. If you are out after that time, if the VC don't get you, the South Vietnamese soldiers guarding us just might shoot first and ask questions later.

"The latrine and our shower are out back on our dock. For God sake do not try to go swimming in the canal. It is full of shit and barbed wire," he said with a scoffing laugh.

"When you get settled, one of us will show you how to use the radio. We have a radio operator now but he is going to transfer out soon and probably won't be replaced, so we will have to do our own transmissions. No classified information is to go over the radio. That kind of stuff will go by courier or when one of us drives into Sa Dec, about 30 clicks west of here."

Clint was thinking of asking a question but the heat seemed to be reducing his reactions. He was sweating profusely. It became apparent that his hyperactive host, who spoke careful English, was not about to give him time to get his thoughts together anyway.

"You will get used to the heat around here. By the way, my name is Glen Rossitor. I am responsible for your performance evaluation. You have a good record, so let's keep it that way.

"As a Phoenix Advisor it is your job to advise the police, make recommendations on public information, monitor the *Chieu Hoi* Program, and identify and neutralize the VCI."

Clint could feel a questioning look come over his own face.

"Don't worry about all this stuff," Rossitor said. "You'll be going to Phoenix Advisor training next week. The training will be a week long in beautiful Vung Tau. It used to be a resort. While the Australians were making it safe for democracy, it got kind of messed up. You will come back smarter and hopefully without any VD. I'll let you finish unpacking; I'm on my way to see the district chief. I'll send Bud in here to talk to you. That is who you're replacing."

Then Rossitor vanished as quickly as he appeared.

A couple minutes later First Lieutenant Bud Swartz sauntered into the room. He was a small man with red hair, ruddy face and buck teeth. He did not look much like an officer, Clint thought.

"Hey, rookie. I'm sure glad you're here. Now I can get the hell out. I'm gone in two weeks and I'm not comin' back. I'm not goin' on anymore patrols even though I'm expected to take you on one. I've made it this long, so I'll be damned if I'm goin' to make myself a target now. What do you want to know about the Phoenix Program?"

"Everything."

"Hell, I don't know everything. Your main job is to count and report on a monthly basis the number of VCI — that's Vietcong Infrastructure — in the district, which is broken down by village and hamlet. Also, never use the word 'assassinate.' We're not assassinating these assholes. We're 'neutralizing' them, or 'liquidating' them, or 'arresting' them. Got it?"

Clint nodded.

"We don't want to break any international treaties. Although we may be tracking these Vietcong leaders, we're not killing them as individuals." Lieutenant Swartz winked.

"How do you count them?" Clint asked.

"Hell, you're the intelligence officer; you figure it out," he said with a chuckle. "I know one thing, if you start out by using my figures you're going to be a failure because I got my numbers down so low now there's no room for improvement. I'm down to six VCI in the whole district. I started out a year ago with about 30 VCI and killed off a few on paper every month, so now it's down to six. You can't go any lower than that. If you write down less than six the higher-ups aren't going to believe you."

"So what do I do?" Clint asked earnestly.

"Just report a new company of Viet Cong moved into the area, so suddenly you now have 29 leaders to track. Then do what I did. Bump off a few every month so you can report improvements are being made.

"And another thing: If you ever do actually identify someone neutralized by name, make a big deal out of it. Also, increase their rank a couple notches; that will look good in your report too."

"What happens to these monthly reports?" Clint asked.

"Oh, they're sent into the province headquarters and intelligence officers there embellish our figures too. Then they send them onto the Corps level where they're made to look even better. Finally they get to the national level and the figures of VC killed look great. Our dumb ass guesses are exaggerated each step along the way, then war policy is made from our phony made-up numbers. That's how we're winning the war . . . on paper."

Clint shook his head in disgust for a moment. He shuffled his feet a little, then a smile came over his face. "I estimate there are at least 31 VCI in my district. The situation suddenly got worse around here."

"You're catching on real fast Lieutenant McGregor. You're going to make a great Phoenix Advisor."

"Question: We're supposed to arrest the VCI we find, right?"

"Yes."

"I hate sounding stupid, but how do we go about doing that?"

"Well, I know you have some military police training," Bud said.

"How do you know that?"

"I'm an intelligence officer."

"Oh, that explains everything."

"You want to know about arresting?"

"Yes."

"Well, in the military police they say you should yell at your suspect, 'You are under arrest.' In the Phoenix Program we shoot them and then tell them they are under arrest."

Clint tried to keep his expression unchanged. "One other question, Bud. What's the deal with the civilian?"

"Aw, he thinks he's in charge of us. But we do pretty much what we want and he's a real tight ass about it. He's been in country for a long time; I know that. He's kind of creepy, if you ask me," Bud said.

"Yeah, but how does he fit in with the chain of command around here?"

"He's not really in charge of us directly and your teammates here are not all in the same chain of command either. The commanding officer for you and me, for example, is in Sa Dec. He rarely comes out here. I let him think it's too dangerous to travel on our one road from Sa Dec."

"But what about Rossitor?"

"He's CIA. You're workin' for the CIA now, buddy."

CHAPTER 6
"You Buy Me Tea?"

Vung Tau, South Vietnam, 1970

Eleven days later Clint found himself in Vung Tau, a city on a small peninsula near Saigon. He sat in a stiflingly hot classroom learning Vietnamese customs, being warned about bar girls who spy for the enemy, practicing combat decision-making and most importantly, discovering the responsibilities of a Phoenix Advisor.

After three days of sitting and sweating and trying to stay awake, Clint was ready for a change of pace. After class some of his classmates suggested checking out the city's nightlife.

Clint and three others, all wearing Army fatigues, piled into a jeep for the short ride to the bar district. They stopped outside a well-lit French Colonial style hotel with a crowded bar next door.

The place was filled with beautiful young Vietnamese women hanging all over American soldiers. Some of the bar girls wore traditional _ao dai_ dress, but most wore tight miniskirts and loose cotton blouses. Clint was rarely intimidated but the scene of such unrestrained lust he observed was a new experience.

A couple of frowning Vietnamese men with holstered pistols stood guard on the steps leading to the open-air bar. The smoke and dust and bare light bulbs with insects fluttering nearby, cast the chaotic scene in a dirty mist.

Clint and his companions, all young company grade officers, sat down at one of the few unoccupied tables.

A sexy girl with a skirt that hardly covered the essentials and long black hair that hung to her waist approached their table. She smiled with lush wet lips.

"We want four beers."

"Make that Vietnamese beer," another said with a southern accent.

"You buy me tea?" the girl asked. "Me want tea."

"Sure, why not? How much does it cost?"

"Two dollar American."

"Sure, go ahead."

Soon a male waiter, of draft-dodger age, arrived with four wet green glass bottles of *bia*. The girl came to the table with a shot glass of brown liquid. Clint wondered if it was tea or actually liquor. He tried to ask but the girl could not understand his question.

"My name Suzy," she said. Then she squeezed herself uninvited into the booth with the four young officers. She put her delicate hand on the thigh of the man next to her. "I do anything you want," she said.

The four men looked at each other and grinned. "I bet you would," one of them said over the din of the crowd.

Then she kissed the man next to her on the neck and tried to put her hand inside his shirt.

"Wow, wait a minute, darlin.' Let's don't rush things," he said.

She drank her tea in two sips. "Me want tea. You buy?" When he delayed she exclaimed, "You no Cheap Cheap Charley! You buy tea."

"OK OK," he said. "You want tea, I'll buy you tea."

"I knew you number one GI," then she skipped to the bar to get some more tea in a very tiny glass. She was back in two minutes but sat next to the soldier on the other end of the U-shaped booth. She drank her tea quickly. With her left hand she grabbed the soldier's crotch and said, "I think you cute. You buy me tea?"

He nearly choked on his beer and said, "Yes, certainly."

"What mean 'certainly'?"

"Means OK."

"OK. I go get tea."

When she departed for the bar, Clint said to his classmates, "All this tea buying is going to get expensive before the night's up."

"Getting felt up by a pretty girl may be worth it."

"Here she comes again. Ask her how much tea costs in Vietnamese money," Clint said.

This time the men scooted over to make room for her at the booth. "How much does tea cost in Vietnamese money?"

"Today, tea cost one-thousand *dong*." The four men were silent for a moment trying to calculate whether this was a fair exchange or not.

The man sitting in the middle next to Clint said, "Quit drinkin' that tea so fast. You're going to a have caffeine fit."

"Look who's talking," one of the men on the end of the booth said. "I've bought two and you haven't bought any."

With that, the little Vietnamese girl practically crawled on top of the table to give the soldier sitting next to Clint a big wet kiss right on the mouth. "You cheap? Or poor?"

Everyone had a good laugh at his expense.

"You sure don't taste like tea. You taste like liquor," he said.

"Maybe tea have *ti ti* what you say."

Clint wondered why everybody at the table had some physical contact with the bar girl except him.

"You GI horny? Want to boom-boom me? Me good. Pay me lot of money, I be good boom-boom."

One of the guys said, "I think for now we're just going to drink our beer."

"OK," she said. "I go boom-boom other GI." With that she threw her arms around the next American soldier who entered the bar.

Suzy was the first young Vietnamese woman Clint had seen up close in the two weeks he had been in the country. All the bar girls were young, he guessed about 18 to 20 years old, all slim and beautiful, and all with long dark hair. He observed the chaotic scene around him. The place was packed with soldiers getting drunk, girls getting sexually aggressive, couples dirty dancing and nasty scowling Vietnamese men looking like they could knife someone at any moment. Across the smoky bar he saw one girl climbing under a table; he looked away, not wanting to see what would happen next. He also noticed one pretty girl who was not being aggressive, but standing at the bar waiting for men to come to her. He asked his companions to let him out of the booth.

Clint walked over to the girl. "How come you didn't come to my table?"

"Me shy," she said looking down.

"What's your name?"

"Suzy."

"What's your real name?" he smiled.

She laughed, "You too smart. Name me Lien."

"Now we're getting somewhere."

"You buy me tea?"

"Sure, OK."

"I have to ask. I no ask, I no eat."

"I'm happy to buy you tea."

"You talk nice," she said with a note of surprise in her voice.

"I do?"

"You like me?" she asked.

"So far."

"So far? What that mean?"

"It means 'Yes.'"

She put her small hand in his and led him to a little metal table with two chairs. He noticed she was very petite, maybe 4 feet 10 inches tall, and probably no more than 90 pounds. He was twice her size.

Clint bought a lot of tea that night and enjoyed every minute of the conversation with the Vietnamese girl.

At about quarter to ten the driver of their jeep corralled the three others and drove them back to their barracks. They shared tales of their experiences with each other on the way. Clint quickly learned he was the only one of the four who did not have some form of sex that night. The last thing he had told Lien was that he would be back tomorrow night. She said she wanted to see him again.

During class the next day Clint thought about the polite little girl with the big brown eyes; eyes that seemed to be saying, *Take me out of here, please.* After hours of classroom instruction he hitched a ride to the bar. As soon as he arrived

Lien came over to him.

"You buy tea now?"

"Yes, and a beer for me too."

"OK," she said and brought the drinks to their table.

Clint was amused at her form of English and they talked for an hour while buying tea and beer.

Finally, Clint got enough courage to ask her to go with him.

"I can no go with you. I have to pay momma-saun to go. You have money to go? I pay momma-saun you money."

"Can we go boom-boom?" Clint asked.

"Yes, we can do that," she said looking embarrassed. "I like you. You treat me nice."

"Where would we go?"

"We go to big house next here," she said.

"The hotel?"

"Yes. You pay momma-saun, you pay guard, and you pay for room. Then we boom-boom. OK, GI?"

"Sounds good to me," he said. "But I think you should start calling me Clint."

"OK, Crint."

He gave her a twenty dollar bill and she went to a room behind the bar.

When she returned, she said, "Momma-saun say we go one hour. No more."

"Well, let's get going then."

"You give me money for guard and house man."

"No, I'll give it to them. You talk for me."

They walked hand-in-hand to the cream colored hotel next door. Lien negotiated prices, and he paid the guard at the gate and the manager of the hotel. She led him up one flight of stairs to a surprisingly large room with a high ceiling. The room was bare except for a mattress on the floor.

Clint noticed how nervous she was. She stood facing him and slipped off her black low-heeled sandals. She looked up at him, and then averted her eyes. She undid her top button.

"Here, let me do that." He slowly released each button until her blouse fell away, exposing a white bra.

Then she walked over to the mattress, unhooked her bra, and slipped off her black satin trousers. With only her white panties on she laid face up on the mattress. When Clint approached, taking off his fatigues as quickly as possible, she put her forearm over her eyes.

He laid down beside her and said, "What's wrong?"

"I shy. I say before. I only be bar girl for three day. This my three day. I have boyfriend before but never do this. You no hurt me?"

Clint thought, *Yeah, that lie is very seductive. I wonder how many times she has given that line.* "Lien, I'm not going to hurt you. We both want this, right?"

She did not say anything in response but she did take her arm from her face. With a curious look she watched him put on a condom.

"Why you do?" she asked. "You need 'cause you sick? Why bring, what you say, balloon?"

Clint had to laugh. "This is not a balloon. This is to keep us from <u>getting</u> sick, not because <u>I am</u> sick. Someone in your position should know these things."

"I tell you, I no do before like this."

Maybe she is telling the truth, Clint thought. He turned

toward her and slipped off her panties. A piece of tissue paper fell out of her underwear and she acted embarrassed all over again.

He just stared at her for a while. She was so small and so pretty that Clint wanted to savor the moment. She was very shapely and only had a very small tuft of straight black pubic hair. The long glossy hair from her head lay across both slim shoulders.

She looked beautiful and innocent and her pleading eyes looked into his. "You like me?" she asked.

"Yes, Lien, very much."

CHAPTER 7

"Free Love?"

Vung Tau, South Vietnam, 1970

Clint hitched a ride to the nightclub the next night and looked for Lien as he had promised her. She was there leaning against the bar. A big smile came over her face when she spotted him.

Lien came over to where he was standing and playfully hit him in the shoulder with her small fist and said, "You come *beaucoup* late. I wait long time see you. I think you no come."

"Why would I miss seeing you? I've been thinking about you all day."

"For sure?"

"Yes, for sure."

"You have to buy something to talk. I no want trouble from momma-saun," Lien said.

"OK, tea for you and a beer for me."

"OK. I get." She pranced away in rhythm to the loud anti-war music.

In a couple minutes she was back with the drinks. They looked into each others eyes for a moment, until Lien looked away, a little embarrassed.

"You number one last night," she said, looking down. "You nice man."

"I like you Lien. I like you a lot," he said, "but why do you work here?"

"I make money. Make more money here than . . . what you say . . . sew clothes. I make money for baby-saun me."

"You have a baby?"

"Yes. I tell you before. I have boyfriend before."

"Where is he?"

"He go away, not come back. I think he die." Lien looked so sad for a moment, Clint was sorry he asked.

"Where's your baby?"

"He with ma of me. I send money."

"Is that a long way from here?"

"Yes, long way. Take bus all day," she said. "But I live close here."

"How close?"

"I go two street, then two other street. Not far."

"Do you have a Vespa or a bicycle?"

"No. I walk."

"When can you leave?"

"Maybe one hour. Too many GI I have stay."

A little later Lien said, "You have to buy more drink now."

"OK, Lien. Here's the money."

"You sit at that table. I be back."

As he waited, he looked over the mad scene of pretty girls, sweating soldiers, the laughing, the groping, the loud music, the glare of the bare light bulbs strung overhead.

Lien returned with the drinks and said, "Here you go GI."

"I thought I told you to call me 'Clint.'"

"OK, Crint. I forget."

"That's OK."

"Crint, me ask you, you come sleep me tonight?"

Surprised, Clint looked at Lien carefully. *Is she a spy?* he wondered. "Can I trust you?"

"*Troi oi!* Crint, what you say? You nice me. I be nice you. I no charge you tonight. You, me . . . what you say? Free love? I free love you."

Clint was torn. He questioned his safety and his sanity when he heard himself say, "Yes, I'll go to your house. But no place else."

"No, just house me. No place other."

After a couple more drinks Lien said she could leave. Then they walked hand-in-hand up the litter strewn sidewalk. There were few people on the street at that hour but those who were there looked at them with disapproving smiles.

They walked by small stores with metal screens locked for the night. Some disabled veterans slept next to the buildings on pieces of cardboard. South Vietnamese soldiers patrolled the dimly lit streets by Jeep. The further they walked from the open-air bar, the quieter and darker it became. After walking three blocks they approached a row of shanties. It appeared that hundreds of squatters had made camp in a previously open field.

"House me, go straight," Lien said.

When they got to her house, Lien grabbed Clint's arm for him to stop. She took a big key from her purse and unlocked the padlock at the doorway. Her house was only about six feet tall and made of scrap planks of wood from ammunition boxes, sheet metal and canvas. A glazed ceramic planter in the shape of an elephant was next to the front door with a single plant growing in it. Cardboard was used for insulation. Clint ducked in the doorway to get into the little house and believed he was seeing how the average Vietnamese lived in the city.

"My house *ti ti*," Lien apologized. "My baby-saun and ma of me live in big house."

"No, this is fine, Lien. Thanks for bringing me here."

"You think me number ten for me bring you here?"

"No, why would I think that?"

"We love too fast?"

"War changes moral standards because people don't know what tomorrow may bring. So we live for the present," Clint expounded, wondering if Lien could understand him.

Lien had a confused look on her face. She seemed to have no idea what Clint was talking about. "OK, what you say."

Her shanty, among a whole block of crowded shanties, was just one room without electricity or running water. Clint noticed pictures torn from magazines of refrigerators, electric stoves, and vacuum cleaners that Lien had pasted on the walls. Two wooden orange crates stood side-by-side to serve as a dresser. The wash basin was metal and sat upon the canvass floor. Hanging beads separated the sleeping area from the rest of the house. The bed, which consisted of a rectangle of foam rubber covered with a white sheet atop a wooden pallet, took nearly half the space of the living quarters. It was even hotter inside the house than outside.

While Lien lit candles and incense sticks, Clint was happy to get his army fatigues off and strip down to his olive drab colored boxer shorts.

"We lay down now?" Lien asked.

"I think that would be a good idea," Clint said as he lay down on the sheet.

"I think good idea too, GI Crint," she said with a little

smile. "I see you want me already."

Lien took off her clothes by candle light, except for her panties, and hung her pink blouse, black satin trousers, and bra on a nail. Clint watched her undress and marveled at how so much beauty could be wrapped into such a small package.

"You want *nouc?*" Lien asked and produced a plastic bottle of water. Clint was not sure about the purity of the warm water but took a couple sips anyway and Lien did the same.

Then Lien pulled the mosquito netting over the bed and lay down beside him. She took his head in her two hands and looked at his face intently. "You nice man Crint," then kissed him fully on the lips. He returned the kiss with enthusiasm.

She slipped her hand into his shorts and said, "You big."

"You beautiful," he said, mocking her abbreviated English.

He kissed her small breasts and could smell the *nouc mam* that Vietnamese used in almost every meal. The musky smell was not offensive to him.

They made love twice that night and once early the next morning. Before he left for class she insisted that she make tea for them on her one-burner kerosene portable stove. She also served some crackers she had stolen from the nightclub.

CHAPTER 8

"And Here is Captain Chuong"

<u>Lap Vo, South Vietnam, 1970</u>

Every night that week Clint stayed with Lien. Every morning he rushed to the Army barracks where he showered, dressed, and made it to class on time. The love-making and the constant heat were exhausting him. During the day he fought to stay awake in the un-air-conditioned classroom and soon learned to sleep with his eyes open.

On the last night in Vung Tau he told Lien it would be his last.

"You go, me go," Lien said.

"I'm going to Lap Vo. Do you know where that is?" Clint asked.

"Me know. Close to baby-saun me. He live An Giang, then big *nouc*, then Lap Vo. Not far," she said with a knowing confident smile.

"I can't take you with me, but we could meet in Lap Vo," he said. "How could we live together? You can't live in the American team compound."

"I smart. I know. I meet you there," she said.

Clint did not know whether to believe her or not. *She could be after my money? Or she could be a VC spy? But she hasn't asked for* money and she never once asked about the war or anything about my assignment. Chances are this is the last I'll ever see her but it would be great if we could set up house in LapVo, he thought. Is my attraction to her more than physical? Why shouldn't two people who're lonely and who enjoy each other's company be together?

The next day a small eight passenger airplane few him to Sa Dec. As the only passenger, he sat in the co-pilot's seat, careful not to touch any of the instruments. The American civilian pilot named some of the places they few over – Dihn Tuong, Kien Hoa, Vinh Long. Finally they landed on a runway, which looked like a cow pasture from the air, in Sa Dec. There he met his commanding officer for the first time and had two days of boring leisure before someone drove from Lap Vo to take him to the district.

The road to Lap Vo in the open-air jeep was a jolting and dusty journey. The roadside vegetation was lush and green, interspersed with canals, and brown thatch roofed shacks built three-to-four feet off the ground. Adults, on foot or riding motor scooters, carried containers of water or packages on their shoulders. Children played games in the street and chickens pecked for seeds and insects.

"Keep your weapon visible and watch for people's hands," the driver said. "You can never be too careful."

"Even the kids?"

"Especially the kids."

Just then a white chicken flew up in the air and Clint instinctively ducked.

"I almost hit something for lunch," the driver said.

"You don't seem to be slowing down any when we're in a village. What happens if you hit one of these chickens?"

"I have to pay for it."

"What if you hit a kid?"

"I have to pay the parents $500."

"Wouldn't it be better just to slow down?"

"No, sir. I don't want to give anyone time to aim. Speed reduces the chance of getting shot."

Clint scooted down in his seat a little.

They arrived at the team house in the heat of the day, their faces streaked with grimy sweat. Clint felt rattled, tired, and stiff as he climbed from the jeep.

The number of team members had declined in the week he had been gone and a few others were getting ready to leave.

Captain Roy and Major Angelo were relaxing in the team house lounge, which also served as a dining room, kitchen, and bar.

Captain Roy, an African American from Detroit, told Clint, "It'll soon be down to just the three of us."

"That's right," Major Angelo, an Italian-American from Rhode Island, agreed. "This'll be just like roommates in college. We'll each do our own thing and not interfere with each other. As far as the team house goes, no one's in charge. If we have to make a decision as to how this place is going to be run we'll decide by consensus." Then he added with a chuckle, "They didn't teach me that at West Point."

"What kinds of decisions?" Clint asked.

"Important stuff," the major said. "Like who's going to Sa Dec to bring back more beer. Or how're we going to arrange the furniture. And, most important, what movies we're going to order from headquarters."

Just then a slender Vietnamese captain quietly walked into

the room.

"And here's Captain Chuong, our local hero," Angelo said brightly. "Lieutenant McGregor, I'd like you to meet Captain Chuong, your counterpart. The two of you're going to work together whether you like it or not."

Clint stood and Chuong quickly extended his hand and said, "I am sure I will like it very much."

"Likewise," Clint said. "Yes, Captain, I look forward to working with you."

Chuong projected a haughty smile; Clint immediately got the impression that the young captain was both arrogant and likeable, two conflicting traits.

"Tomorrow I'll introduce you to Colonel Hu," Chuong said. "He plans on meeting us at 1100 hours. Be sure to wear your best uniform."

Clint had not heard of Colonel Hu but got the impression he was important. Clint was impressed with the captain's command of the English language. He talked slowly, clearly and formally.

As if Angelo were reading Clint's mind, he interjected, "Yes, Colonel Hu's an influential person around here. Captain Chuong may not agree with my description but I call Hu one of the last remaining warlords. When he speaks thousands of his followers listen. That's why we paid him to be on our side."

"We what?" Clint asked, feeling naïve.

"We paid him a million dollars in gold to be on our side. It was a damn good investment too. I think we could win this war quickly and cheaply if we just paid off all the regional leaders," Angelo expounded.

"I would not know anything about this," Chuong said.

"Just like back home," Captain Roy said, "The Golden Rule: whoever has the gold, rules."

"That I do know something about," Chuong said. "Lieutenant, I will be here tomorrow at 1000 hours to take you to the Hu Compound. You will meet him and many other leaders you need to know. You will not be expected to say anything except that you are glad to meet whoever you talk to. Most of them will not know what you are saying anyway; just smile a lot. Colonel Hu will know everything you say and maybe some things you are thinking too. I have some other business to attend to, so I will go now." And he left quickly before anyone had a chance to thank him for coming.

After the screen door to the team house slammed, Angelo said, "Chuong's an interesting character. He's a serious and dedicated man. And a cold and calculating son-of-a-bitch. Once he lived with the enemy for six months, gained their confidence, and walked an entire company into a deadly ambush. He's one of the few Vietnamese I've ever met who has a feeling of patriotism for his country. If we win this war, he could advance rapidly within the military or government. If we get run out of here, he'll be one of the first to be arrested and executed. He's a man on the way up or one of the many minor leaders massacred if the communists take over.

"You can take my interpreter with you tomorrow. He'll keep you informed as to what's going on at your meeting with Hu. You can trust him. His name is Sergeant Binh."

The next morning Clint dressed as well as he could under the circumstances, wishing he had an iron to put some pleats in his pants. Chuong made his appearance exactly on time and gave a disapproving glance at Clint's dress. Shortly later

Sergeant Binh arrived.

Upon seeing Binh, Captain Chuong said, "It will not be necessary for him to come with us. I can interpret."

Angelo interjected. "I've asked that Sergeant Binh accompany Lieutenant McGregor. He will also be driving our Jeep, Captain."

"Yes sir," Chuong said, not showing any expression.

CHAPTER 9

"Communists have no religion."

Lap Vo, South Vietnam, 1970

Sergeant Binh drove fast, scaring chickens and children out of the way in a swirl of dust on the pitted roadway. He managed to hit every pot hole without slowing. In the backseat of the Jeep were his passengers. Clint held on for dear life while Chuong scanned the passing countryside for snipers and acted unfazed by the jolting ride.

Suddenly Binh swerved to the right down a dirt road and came to a clearing, then to a heavily fortified compound. As he slid to a stop, guns pointed at the Jeep from all directions. Binh talked rapidly in Vietnamese to the menacing guards. Clint was nervous but Chuong looked arrogantly ahead with a slight scowl.

After an assertive exchange, Binh turned toward his passengers and said, "We can go now." Chuong nodded, the metal gate opened, and the guards saluted. Chuong returned the salute in a disdainful manner. Clint's heartbeat returned to normal.

Inside the compound Binh drove in a more normal manner and parked next to a line of Jeeps already present.

Chuong said something to Binh. In English, Binh told Clint, "OK, we get out now. Follow Captain Chuong." Clint realized Binh was not translating for Chuong at that moment, but simply giving helpful advice.

They entered a building with an ornately carved door where two Vietnamese soldiers stood at attention at either side of the doorway.

Chuong, with Clint following, entered a large room with a huge low table in the center. Seated on the polished floor at the table were mostly middle aged and older Vietnamese men, some with grey beards. About half were in military uniform while others wore black slacks and white dress shirts open at the collar.

"We are a little early," Chuong said to Clint in English. "More will be coming. When more get here I will introduce you."

Over the next twenty minutes others arrived and took their seats. At each place setting was a water glass filled with what appeared to be discolored water.

With the meeting time approaching Chuong began introducing Clint to those seated as they slowly walked around the table. Most stood to meet him with a smile and firm handshake. Some of the elderly men stayed seated and reached up to shake his hand. The younger men bowed slightly with their hands together before taking Clint's hand. All seemed happy to meet him; Clint was surprised at the deference shown him. Chuong spoke only in Vietnamese but Clint was amazed that his counterpart seemed to know the name of each man at the table, about thirty in all.

Clint also noticed the pretty young women in white satin standing silently against the walls of the room.

The time for the meeting came and passed. No one seemed

concerned and spoke quietly with each other.

Then Colonel Hu made a grand entrance into the large room with a broad smile on his round face, about twenty minutes past the designated time for the meeting. His uniform was perfectly pressed and ribbons covered much of the left side of his chest. Everyone stood to applaud, nod, and smile at him.

As the applause dissipated, Hu said something. Behind Clint a voice said, "Thank you so much. Thank you for coming today. Please all be seated." It was Sergeant Binh, the interpreter, who Clint had nearly forgotten about.

All took their seats. After a few minutes Hu stood and raised his glass. All the attendees quickly came to their feet. With his glass raised at arm's length, Hu spoke and Binh translated, "Gentlemen, please join me in a salute to a free Vietnam. May we prevail and stop the killing of our innocent people by the northerners and their lackeys."

Everyone took a drink from their water glass. And all said something in Vietnamese that Clint did not understand but assumed was a sign of agreement. Then they all sat down quietly.

"What is this drink?" Clint asked.

Binh said "Cognac."

Not straight cognac, Clint realized, but a cognac highball. It was actually quite refreshing, he thought.

The women who had been standing quietly on the perimeter began bringing out platters of chopped chicken, spicy noodles, cooked greens, and other items Clint did not recognize. The ladies were also quick to keep every glass filled. Clint made a determined effort to use his chopsticks.

The hum of visiting friends and allies filled the room. Neither Chuong nor Clint said much. Binh did not sit at the table but squatted comfortably nearby. Some of the other men at the table also had aides that squatted behind them.

The drinking, eating, and visiting seemed to be enjoyed by all. This went on for an hour.

Then Hu stood and raised his hand and the noise immediately ceased.

Binh quietly translated: "Again, I thank you gentlemen for attending today. We will not have a long meeting today. Feel free to continue to enjoy your drink."

Food was pushed away and the glasses brought closer.

"I want to thank you for making our district one of the safest in the country. Our hard work and loyalty is paying off. We thank the Americans for being our good allies. Their aid is important to us, and we must use their support wisely, but it is us who have to win the war and the peace to follow.

"We can never forget that Ho Chi Minh killed our great Hoa Hao prophet, Huyhn Phu So, our native son of the Mekong Delta. Communists have no religion. Without religion we will only be dust when we die. Our spirit will be killed along with our bodies. Without religion there will be no restoration. Without religion we are only a thought and of no substance. Without religion we shall truly parish for all eternity.

"The North Vietnamese look down their noses at us. They think we are all ignorant peasants. They think we are all uneducated. They think we are no better than Cambodians." That comment received a light chuckle. "They will see how wrong they are.

"The founders of our traditions are living Buddhas,

destined to save mankind from suffering and to protect the Vietnamese nation. It is our duty to aid the poor. Helping the poor is more important than building pagodas, giving food offerings, or conducting elaborate ceremonies.

"Our good work to help our people is not enough. As we labor to advance education, healthcare, and the economy it is wasted effort if we tolerate instability, corruption, and disorder. Sometimes we must be brutal in order to allow fairness for advancement.

"We need to live and fight smart. When we get U.S. aid we must not take it for our personal projects, but for the projects for the common good. We should not appropriate the bricks, nor dilute the cement with sand, nor levy too high a tax to transport these items.

"That is all I have to say about that for now. You do what I say and you will be my friend. If you do not help the people, but help only yourself, then you are not my friend, you are my enemy. I will know if you are friend or enemy. My inspectors will tell me.

"You know how I feel. I support my friends and I punish my enemies." With that said, the men around the table cheered and slapped the table.

"We have a special guest today. He is from the United States. He is a young man but he is wise. He will help us get aid from America. He will help me punish our enemies." Clint did not know Hu was talking about him until he saw the men at the table turn their heads toward him, smile, and nod.

Clint began to feel uncomfortable because he did not know what was expected of him.

"You stay seated until I tell you to get up," Chuong said

quietly, sitting beside him.

Hu continued talking and Binh continued translating: "Lieutenant McGregor is our new Phoenix Advisor. You are to provide him with information about our enemies in your villages and hamlets. You are to make sure he travels without harm in your villages and hamlets. He will come to your village every month. You let him know what aid you need. He will let his leaders in Sa Dec City know what we need and want.

"I have a special presentation to make to our new Phoenix Advisor. It is a symbol of our alliance and the trust I put in him."

"Now you stand up," Chuong said.

"Please come forward, Lieutenant McGregor," Binh interpreted.

Hu was holding a small .38 caliber pistol in the air. Clint quickly recalled the Vietnamese etiquette he learned training in Vung Tau the week before. As he rose, he was careful not to show the soles of his boots to anyone. He walked forward to Colonel Hu and when he reached the head of the table, he bowed with his hands meeting as if in prayer. Hu offered him the pistol and Clint extended both his hands with the palms up. Hu handed him the pistol and Clint took it in both hands and made another quick bow with a smile. Hu then extended his right hand and the two men shook hands. Those sitting around the big table applauded.

When Clint returned to his seat Chuong said to him quietly, "You must return the pistol to Colonel Hu before you leave the country."

Clint looked at the pistol. It was old and corroded. It probably had not been fired in years. Clint told himself that he would never fire it unless absolutely necessary. It looked like it could explode if the trigger were pulled.

He slipped it into his belt. Clint noticed that most of the men in the room were still looking at him with approval. He did not feel worthy of such honors but felt welcomed and somehow indebted to Colonel Hu.

Hu was still talking but Clint was lost in thought and was not paying attention even though Binh continued to translate.

Then the young ladies started delivering tiny glasses of a clear liquid to each man. When all had been served, Colonel Hu spoke English for the first time. He said, "Hundred percent," and gulped the liquor in one swallow. All the men followed and repeated, "Hundred percent," and threw back their drinks. Clint did the same. The liquor scorched the back of his throat and instantly made his insides feel very warm. The ladies filled the glasses again. This time Clint tried to sip the drink but found that it burned his lips and tongue. *No wonder they gulp it. This is pure alcohol*, he said to himself, and swigged the rest of it.

Binh leaned in and said, "It is rice alcohol." Then he gave the Vietnamese name of the drink, *"Ba Xi De."*

"What did you say it's called?" Clint asked.

"Remember it like English. Say 'Ba – See – Day.'"

"I've got it," Clint said.

"Don't drink too much," Captain Chuong warned.

"I can understand why," Clint said, feeling warm all over and his disposition rapidly changing to a state of relaxation.

Hu shook some hands at the head of the table and departed quickly. A few minutes later the high ranking officers left, followed by their aides.

Chuong turned to Clint and said, "OK. We go now."

On the way back to the team house Clint held onto his seat tightly to keep from being thrown from the Jeep but his thoughts were still on the meeting. *What am I, some kind of local celebrity now? I don't know a thing about foreign aid. That was not covered in my training. Captain Roy advises on agriculture. The major has something to do with foreign aid, I think. I'll have to ask him.*

On the shoulder of the road ahead a young woman was carrying a basket on her arm. Walking flatfooted in sandals, her slim hips swayed while her long straight hair swung in unison in the opposition direction.

It looks like Lien. When they passed he looked back at her. Her face was of a lighter skin tone and more angular. Her eyes look sad. She was pretty but it was not Lien.

Will I ever see Lien again? What will happen to her?

He felt lonely.

CHAPTER 10
"What Kind of War is This?"

Long Hung Village, South Vietnam, 1970

The next day Captain Chuong informed Clint, "Tomorrow we are going to 'win hearts and minds.'"

The Vietnamese Captain, usually a very serious young man, had a good laugh at his own comment. Evidently he had been reading American propaganda or listening to President Nixon's speeches, Clint thought.

"What're we going to do?"

"We are going to drive to Long Hung Village in your Jeep, if that is OK, and meet with local leaders. We have public aid to distribute to hamlets in the village."

"How much money or supplies we talking about?"

"We can tell them we have 75,000 *dong* for them. Some goes to each of the three hamlets in the village but they have to decide how to use the money before they get any of it."

Early the next morning Clint, Chuong, and Binh met at the Jeep parked in front of the team house. Each man carried a M16 assault rifle. The sun was just over the misty horizon and it was already hot outside.

"You are going to see some of the rural area today," Chuong said.

"I thought this was the rural area," Clint said.

"You have not seen people this dirty and ignorant and poor

before. When we get to the Long Hung village headquarters, the road does not go any further. From there all travel is either on foot or by sampan."

"Sounds interesting."

With Chuong giving directions to the village, Binh made a haphazard attempt to miss the pot holes. After an hour of driving, over what would be considered crude hiking trails in the U.S., the three arrived at the entrance to the village without incident. Clint, with muscles aching from the rough ride, was happy to get out of the Jeep.

No sooner had Clint touched his feet on the ground when he was surrounded by a swarm of children yelling at him and pushing each other for a chance to touch him. They hollered "*My*" for American and "chocolate." They also yelled the international word, "OK" over and over again.

Clint felt like a hundred insects were stinging his arms. Then he realized the half-naked kids were pulling the hair on his forearms.

Binh, who was standing next to him, said, "They want the hair on your arms. Vietnamese don't have hairy arms."

Just then a thin man with a grey beard ran up to them, shouted at the children and shooed them away. The wide-eyed kids retreated about 20 yards but continued to gawk at the strange looking human being in green fatigues and a boonie hat.

"Some have never seen an American before," Binh said.

The village elder, wearing dark slacks and a white short sleeved shirt, bowed to the American and apologized in Vietnamese for the rude behavior of the children. Then he shook hands with all three. Inviting them to the village center, he motioned with his arm to a tin covered outdoor table in the shade, already set with tea service. They met two other village leaders at the table.

Although impolite in Vietnamese culture, Chuong impatiently wasted no time on small talk before starting the meeting. Clint noted that Binh could not interpret everything because he did not want to interrupt. Clint had already been briefed on the main purpose of the gathering, so had a basic understanding of the meeting's purpose anyway.

As the meeting proceeded, Chuong appeared to be getting irritated and more impatient. Binh explained to Clint that the hamlet leaders did not attend the meeting as expected. The village chief apologetically explained that one of the hamlet leaders was at a conference in Sa Dec, one was sick at home, and another decided it was more important to tend to his rice paddy. The village officials seemed embarrassed but there was nothing they could do about the missing hamlet chiefs.

The meeting ended with outward pleasantries but Clint noted that Chuong could barely contain his disappointment. Clint had lots of question that he thought better to ask later.

Chuong said, "We are going to visit a Popular Forces outpost now. It is going to be a long hot walk to get there. Do you have water with you?" Both Clint and Binh nodded.

Chuong asked for volunteers to guard the Jeep. He paid two children who quickly stepped forward. "Do not allow anyone to touch the Jeep or steal the gas. I will pay you more when I get back if I am satisfied with your work. Do you understand?"

The two shirtless boys smiled and nodded.

After a few yards down the trail into the jungle Clint asked, "What happened at the meeting?"

"They all knew this was an important meeting," Chuong said. "They had plenty of notice. The aid cannot be distributed unless all the local leaders agree on how it is to be spent. We are trying to teach them leadership and democracy too. It is not just the money."

"The people were not there to make a decision," Binh added.

Then Chuong said something to Binh in Vietnamese.

"Captain Chuong called them cowards for not coming to the meeting," Binh said to Clint.

"Why?"

"If they took American aid the Viet Cong may punish them. They were afraid to look like they were on our side," Binh said.

That is when Clint began to realize that Binh was willing to provide more analytical information than Chuong. Evidently, Binh recognized that he worked for the Americans and not for Chuong. He was not just a translator, but an interpreter.

Chuong said, "Now we are going to see some people who are brave."

The three hiked several miles on vine and palm shrouded trails. Every fifty yards or so they approached a hooch next to a mucky little canal. Chuong and Binh talked to the peasants in Vietnamese and asked them if the VC were bothering them. The residents all bowed and smiled and said they felt safe. Their children shouted "OK" when they saw the American.

Clint noticed that whenever the meeting was cordial, which was almost always the case, the women would approach him and take hold of his hands. "Why do they touch my hands?" he asked.

Binh said, "They want to know if you are an officer. If you

are an officer your hands will be smooth. If you are not an officer your hands will be rough from doing physical labor."

Clint put his hands together and had to conclude, *Yes. They are quite soft.*

Over every little stream a "monkey bridge" made of bamboo was built. They were obviously constructed for small people, not someone Clint's size. His weight made the tiny footbridges groan and shake. Inevitably, one of the rickety bridges could not hold him. The bridged trembled under his weight, began to lean precariously to one side, and buckled. Clint attempted to move quickly to the other end of the bridge, which only hastened its collapse. He crashed through the bridge, fell a couple feet to the brown water, and dropped his rifle into the muck.

He was surprised to no longer be holding his rifle. Suddenly naked and panicky without his weapon, he had no choice but to hold his breath and duck into the polluted water to retrieve it. After feeling around in the mud, he finally felt something hard buried in the thick slime and he pulled the gun to the surface. A stream of swill emanated from the barrel. With the locally crafted bridge now a pile of sticks pointing in every direction, Clint waded to shore to the delight of a couple peasants who were watching.

"I think I just made some more VC by destroying their bridge," Clint said. Binh laughed and Chuong looked disgusted.

Once ashore Clint discovered several leaches attached to his forearms where his sleeves had been rolled up. He took a minute to pull them off. Little rivulets of blood trickled down his arms once the engorged pests were plucked.

As they went deeper into the jungle Chuong said, "There

is VC here but the people won't tell us. They don't want us to bring troops here and start a battle. The VC controls this area by night and we control the area in the daylight."

"Is it dangerous here?" Clint asked.

Chuong scoffed, "Of course. You brought your rifle didn't you?"

"It's so damn dirty now I'm not sure I'd want to fire it."

After arduous trekking they began to see evidence that they were nearing their destination, the Popular Forces Outpost Number 106 on the Van Dinh canal. Along the trail they began to spot laundry of every descriptions hanging in the limbs to dry.

When Clint saw some bras hanging from branches, he asked, "Are we coming to an army post or a nudist colony?"

Binh replied, "Some of the soldiers bring their wives and children with them."

When they approached the outpost no one seemed to be on guard duty. The three just walked up to the fence surrounding the fort without being challenged. The outpost was made of straw and compacted mud. It reminded Clint of something appropriate for a fort in the American frontier west.

Binh yelled at someone sitting on a rock who was visible from the fence line. The startled soldier took off running into a thatched roof building. A moment later an officer in army uniform, with his shirt tail hanging out, and wearing flip flops on his feet, hustled to the perimeter to greet them.

Captain Chuong said something to the disheveled officer and the officer saluted; Chuong returned the salute. They talked to each other for awhile and then the PF officer asked Chuong if he wanted a tour of the facility.

"Of course we do. We did not come here to walk in the sun for our health."

It was quickly apparent to Clint that the living conditions were abysmal. The bunkers, rooms, and floors were basically molded dirt. The fence surrounding the fort was made of tree limbs and barbed wire. *This might be considered a hippie commune if it were in the United States*, he thought.

Chuong questioned the young officer severely and he nervously responded.

Binh summarized the discussion for Clint: "There are 35 men in this compound and a number have brought their families. Their job is to guard the canal. Anyone using the canal is required to check in at the outpost. If they don't they may be shot."

That is when Clint noticed the guard tower with two men holding rifles.

Clint thought the fort was dismal, filthy, cramped, and depressing.

Clint interpreted Chuong's facial expression as one of disgust. He said to Clint, "I told you I would show you some brave people. I did not tell you they live like pigs."

After they finished their tour of the facility, Chuong said, "I want to see another area before we return to Long Hung."

The three crossed a rice field where the farmer and his sons were tilling by hand. An old woman was smashing dry dirt clods with a heavy long handled mallet. The farmer yelled that he wanted seed to plant.

Chuong said, "Don't pay any attention to him. He's crazy."

Walking along a ditch, uncomfortable at being in the open, they arrived at Muong Dao canal. Soon they were in the jungle again and feeling safer from snipers. All along the way the three stopped at hutches and talked to the people.

One old woman complained that the Army drafted their school teacher and now the children cannot go to school. Chuong tried to explain to her that she needed to apply to the government for a teacher and one would be provided.

She laughed at Chuong with her betel leaf stained teeth and said the government would not do anything for the people.

"People here are so dumb," Chuong said in English.

Clint noticed that every cluster of hutches had a water hole. When he asked about them Binh simply said they were "fish ponds." Clint wondered what they fed the fish but he soon learned when he saw a young girl run to an outhouse that over hung the pond.

It was mid-afternoon and the water in their canteens had turned hot and unpleasant. At one hooch Chuong asked for tea. The family rushed around and quickly gave little cups to each of them and the wife poured steaming tea into them. The muddy water taste overwhelmed the taste of the tea. Next the polite family served watermelon, which was sweet and juicy but warm. The skinny husband with rotting teeth seemed to welcome the company and talked in a very hospitable manner. When the watermelon was consumed he offered everyone some snuff from a red can but all declined with grace, so he took some himself. The pause in their travel was welcome but they needed to continue in order to get back to Lap Vo before dark.

After about 30 yards down the trail Chuong said, "That man is VC. I hope he did not poison us."

They passed more small hutches, single women with dirty

children, crippled old men with stringy grey beards, and old ladies spitting bright orange areca-nut and betel leaf juice on the ground. The poverty was beyond imagination for Clint. He remembered that Lien had pasted magazine advertisements on her walls as decoration; he doubted these people could afford such a luxury.

Around a bend in the trail, all three stopped in amazement at what they saw. At the edge of a clearing was a new large green John Deere tractor. A young man lay on the ground in the shade next to the machine.

Chuong walked up and booted the slumbering young man in the ass and asked, "Who owns this tractor and all this land?"

Startled from his nap, the youth with slicked back dark hair pointed to a middle-age man with a thin white jacket and a colorful scarf around his neck on the other side of the little canal.

The man waved to them in the typical Vietnamese manner with the palm down. He jumped into a small sampan, polled himself across and stepped ashore in a deferential manner.

Chuong asked him, "Who owns all this?"

"I do," the man said with pride.

"And how old is your worker?"

"He is seventeen."

Some more discussion followed but the man talked so fast Binh could not translate all of it. The man said he owned the tractor and 10 hectors of land (25 acres) and paid 700,000 piasters ($6,000) for the tractor. He said he ran the tractor day and night for his relatives and neighbors who pay him. He also said his taxes were very high. As he talked, Clint noted paper money bulging from the front pockets of his jacket.

Once down the trail again, Chuong said, "That son-of-a-bitch is a liar. That worker is not seventeen. He is a draft dodger. You would be surprised how many seventeen year old boys are married to twenty-six year old women. And if he is running his tractor day and night, he is paying off the VC. And he does not pay any taxes. The government is afraid to come out here to collect taxes."

Tired of walking, Chuong hired a sampan to take them back to Long Hung village.

Clint felt lost in the maze of interconnected canals but Chuong seemed confident they where headed in the right direction. In the little row boat the three passengers remained quiet in order to bring little attention to themselves from anyone who may see them from the shore.

When they arrived in the village the two boys, with toy rifles over their shoulders, were still guarding the Jeep. Clint shook their hands and they looked both proud and embarrassed. Chuong, after inspecting the vehicle, handed them a few more paper bills.

On the Jeep ride back, Clint felt exhausted. He was thinking about drinking beer, and taking a shower, even though the water would come from the polluted river.

They arrived in Lap Vo just before dark, their clothes soaked with perspiration.

Upon arriving at the team house in the Jeep, Captain Roy ran up to them and exclaimed, "The VC just robbed the candy store!"

"What kind of war is this?" Clint laughed.

CHAPTER 11

"That's democracy for you"

Hoi An Dong Village, 1970

A week later two beings came into the life of the team house — a scruffy young dog and a scruffy young translator. That made one team house dog and three translators.

How the dog avoided the guards and the concertina wire at the perimeter of the compound was a mystery. The middle-sized long-haired black dog walked right into the team house lounge where everyone was sitting having coffee or a smoke after breakfast. He quietly appeared, looked at each of the four remaining team house members, and walked up to Clint, who was sitting on a couch. The dog promptly drooled on his sandaled feet. Clint jerked his feet back while the others had a good laugh.

The smile on Mr. Rossitor's face, however, faded quickly. "Get that filthy animal out of here!"

Captain Roy said, "No, let him stay."

"He looks hungry," protested Major Angelo.

"I'll get him some water," Clint said as he jumped up, found a bowl and poured the poor animal some water out of a plastic jug.

"Don't be wasting our water," Rossitor said. "Let him drink out of the canal."

"That water's full of shit," Clint responded.

"You bathe in it every day," Rossitor said.

"Yes, but I keep my mouth closed," Clint said, getting a little irritated.

"Where's he going to sleep?" Rossitor asked, even though the officers were no longer paying any heed to his demands because he was leaving in a couple weeks.

"He'll sleep with me," Clint protectively volunteered.

"He's going to bring fleas into this place," Rossitor warned.

"We've got fleas already," Clint said.

Captain Roy added to the exchange. "We've got some flea powder around here someplace. It's in a green can." He started looking in the kitchen cupboards.

"Everything's in a green can around here," Angelo said. "If we stay here long enough even our shit will be olive drab."

"Isn't that the normal color?" Roy said with a big white smile.

Rossitor, disgusted, started to leave the room, and then stopped. "Oh, Clint, your new interpreter is going to arrive soon. He'll be here in a couple minutes."

"That's great," Clint said, appreciative, because he would no longer have to share Binh's services with Major Angelo. Then added, "Is that a couple minutes American time or Vietnamese time?"

"What do you think?" Rossitor responded with a snarl. "And another thing: Tomorrow we're going to visit a village and I want you and your new interpreter to come along."

"OK, what time?"

"We'll leave here at 0800 hours."

"That cuts into my beauty rest but I'll be ready."

"And get into some kind of uniform. Look like an American

Army officer," Rossitor added.

"You don't like my black pajamas?"

"You look like the Viet Cong." Rossitor went to his office carrying a notebook.

A half-hour later Sergeant Binh came into the team house with a skinny young man wearing a dark green uniform with no insignia. "Lieutenant McGregor, this is Phuc, your new interpreter."

Phuc bowed, then took one look at the dog and said something to Sergeant Binh.

"What'd he say?" Clint asked Binh.

"Phuc said that black dogs are the best kind to eat."

"No one will eat my dog, and that's an order!"

Roy and Angelo roared with laughter. Phuc looked confused.

Clint soon learned the new interpreter knew little English. His father paid a bribe to keep his son out of the Army by buying him a position as an interpreter.

The next morning Rossitor walked into the lounge right on time where Clint was waiting for him.

"Where's Phuc?" Rossitor asked.

"I don't know," Clint responded.

"Why don't you know? He's your interpreter."

Clint began to defend himself. "I just met him yesterday. I have no idea where he lives . . ." Then he gave up the defense and poured himself another cup of coffee.

For the next half hour Rossitor paced the floor and Clint tried to stay out of his way.

Finally Phuc arrived. Rossitor yelled at him in Vietnamese and pointed at his watch. Phuc grinned and bowed in a submissive manner.

Then Rossitor took a water proof map from his canvass satchel and pointed out Hoi An Dong village. "This village is having a meeting today to discuss their annual projects. The government will provide 550,000 p. if they can match this amount of money with 125,000 p."

"How are the villagers expected to come up with that kind of match?" Clint asked.

Rossitor said, "It's understood they cannot come up with much money, so they will be given credit for labor and any supplies that may be donated. We are just going there today to make sure these projects are selected in a democratic manner. This is called a 'village self-development meeting.' But first we have to get there. There're no roads to this place, just trails, so we can't take the Jeep. We're going to walk to the market and see if we can get some rides on motor scooters."

The three walked the quarter mile to the market and began asking idle young men with motor scooters if they could give them a ride. When Rossitor began waving some money around several villagers volunteered to take him and Phuc but not Clint.

Clint wondered what the problem was and asked Phuc.

In his best English, Phuc stuttered, "You fat. Tire go flat."

The villagers, who crowded around, thought this was hilarious. They laughed, pointed at Clint and then the back tires of the little scooters. Finally one driver stepped forward with his Honda and said he would take Clint on the back of his scooter. But Rossitor objected when he learned the driver wanted to be paid twice the rate as the other two drivers.

Rossitor said in Vietnamese, "Everyone cost the same or

none of us go."

The Honda owner backed down and agreed to take Clint at the same rate as the others. The villagers were still laughing when the smoky little machines sped through town and then onto a jungle trail.

They arrived at their destination after a half hour of being slapped by wet leaves along the trail, fording mud holes, and fighting off biting inspects. The three were met by the village chief, the deputy for security, and the police chief. With handshakes, bows, and the offer of cigarettes they were warmly greeted. They pointed out the meeting spot where 50 people were already assembled at an outdoor café. The villagers looked at the two Americans with curiosity.

Before the meeting started the village chief told Rossitor that he was very upset.

"What's wrong?" Rossitor asked.

The village chief quietly told Rossitor he would not be village chief next month.

"Why?"

"The voters ganged up on me, so I didn't get the most votes. It wasn't fair."

Rossitor said he was sorry for the bad news and explained, "It happens all the time in America."

The chief looked confused.

Then Rossitor explained to Clint the concern being discussed.

Clint responded, "That's democracy for you."

The lame duck village chief started the meeting. Soon both men and women stood and took turns making impassioned little speeches. Clint could not understand much of what was being said and Phuc was unable to translate.

During a brief break in the meeting Rossitor quietly explained that each person was advocating for the project they wanted financed. "Later they will vote on all the projects and the one that gets the most votes will be funded. Others may be funded in priority order based on the number of votes if any money is left after the leading project is funded."

"That sounds simple enough," Clint responded.

After hours of debate they voted by raising there hands. The number one project was the purchase of three Rototillers for the village. Second was a maternity clinic, third a water pump, and last was an irrigation ditch with a footbridge.

By then it was close to dinner time, so the women ran home to prepare the evening meal while men hung around the village square smoking and visiting.

Rossitor, Clint, and Phuc found their drivers and headed back to Lap Vo in a motorized single file through the thick jungle.

Clint felt satisfied that the villagers learned something about democracy and self-government that day.

CHAPTER 12

"You happy see me?"

Lap Vo, South Vietnam, 1970

Nearly a week later Clint McGregor lay in bed listening to the distant bombing in Cambodia; the bombing President Nixon said was not taking place. Clint was exhausted, having just survived another of Rossitor's forced jungle marches. The first half of the tour was easy enough. They went to My An Hung village as paying passengers on the rear of Honda motor scooters.

It was the return trip that nearly gave Clint heat stroke. Rossitor wanted to take a different route back to Lap Vo. They walked 12 miles in the hot and humid jungle on leaf shrouded trails too narrow for motorbikes.

They inspected Popular Forces outposts on the way. Like the National Guard in the U.S., the PF soldiers usually operated close to their homes. Just like the PF outpost Clint inspected with Captain Chuong, these forts were nothing more than mud huts surrounded by barbed wire.

"These poor soldiers could be overrun by the VC anytime they chose," Rossitor said. "They're required to go on patrol but they tend to operate in areas where they know it's unlikely they'd run into any VC. Hell, neither side in this area wants to have a gun fight, so they try not to bump into each other.

"One of the problems with PF security," Rossitor explained,

"is that traditionally soldiers don't do construction in Vietnam, it's beneath their dignity. So, villagers are drafted to build their outposts. Therefore, the Viet Cong have the building plans for each fort and know the weak points and fields of fire."

On the long trail back, Rossitor and Clint stopped at each outpost, talked to the leaders, inspected their security plans, made suggestions, and walked to the next outpost while being guarded by the PF soldiers until they joined up with the soldiers at the next outpost.

"Asking questions of Vietnamese, whether soldier or civilian, is an exercise in futility," Rossitor had said. "They normally try to answer questions, particularly from outsiders, with the answer they think the questioner wants to hear. In their culture this isn't lying, it's being polite."

As Clint thought about his latest exhausting experience he threw his sheet off. On this night even a single cotton sheet was too hot to lie beneath.

He recalled with a smile one particular civilian they talked to on the trail who was uncharacteristically forthright. According to Rossitor the peasant said, "Why should we get rid of the VC as long as they don't make trouble? The government helps us because they want us to support the government and not the VC. Would the government care about us if there were no VC?"

Clint remembered how anxious the people standing near this one honest peasant became. One person tried to get him to shut up while others moved away from him.

When morning finally came Clint showered, ate breakfast, and anticipated a day of leisure.

Unexpectedly, a South Vietnamese soldier, who had been

on guard with others at the entrance to the compound, came to the front door of the team house. When he tried to enter the building Sergeant Binh stopped him.

Clint heard the commotion at the front door and Phuc, who was lounging nearby, tried to interpret for him: "Binh say, what do here; no you go; stop him. He have message. What. *Co dep* at gate. See you."

Just what I need, a draft dodger for a translator, Clint thought.

Binh stood with his hands on his hips while the soldier walked back to his post.

Binh then walked toward the common lounge area of the team house. "Lieutenant McGregor . . . oh, there you are. There is a girl at the gate who wants to see you."

"There is?" Clint said, not expecting a visitor. He thought of a "girl" as a child, not a young woman. Then he realized, *It must be Lien. I didn't think I'd see her again.*

Clint wanted to run the hundred yards to the front gate, but thought it best to show some dignity in front of the Vietnamese enlisted men. He walked briskly instead. There she stood, just outside the compound being gawked at by the guards. When she saw Clint she displayed a beautiful smile. Her long black hair hung on both sides of her delicate face. She wore a pink short sleeved blouse with a print pattern, long black satin trousers, shiny black high heeled sandals, and held a multi-colored striped parasol. Her delicate fingers were well manicured and she wore a white beaded bracelet on her right wrist. With her dark pink lipstick she was immediately identified as a city girl, not from the village.

Clint made his way through the gate and greeted her in

a formal manner, first with a little bow and then dared to shake her hand. He knew public displays of affection with the opposite sex were taboo, particularly in a conservative rural village like Lap Vo.

"You look big eye," she said. "You no think I come? I tell you I come. You still want me? You happy see me?"

"Yes, Lien. Yes."

"I have house. You come with me now?" she asked.

"Yes, I can come with you. Where do you live?"

"You see house me?" She pointed to a newly constructed duplex three hutches down and across the street.

"You're very close," he said.

"You come with me now," she said.

They walked together on the side of the dusty street, knowing the Vietnamese gate guards were staring at them and speaking quietly to each other. Clint thought to himself, *She is by far the most beautiful woman in the village.*

When they got to the little duplex, they walked up a wooden plank to the front door on the right side of the small sturdy building on stilts. Lien took a key from her purse and unlocked the padlock. Once inside and the door shut behind them, they embraced for a long time. He felt himself getting aroused and Lien squeezed him tighter.

"Yes, you happy to see me," she said with a laugh. She grabbed his butt and pulled him even closer to her. "Yes, me think you *beaucoup* happy see me."

The apartment was one room divided front from back by a curtain made of pink and blue vertical strips of plastic. The front room was a living area furnished only with a hammock and one white plastic chair. The back room, which opened onto a small canal, was for sleeping, cooking and eating. It had a wide wooden sleeping pallet with a cushion. With the padding removed it doubled as a low dining table. Near the back doorway sat a little one burner gas stove.

"You bought this house?" he asked.

"Yes, I buy half year," she said.

"You mean you rented it."

"Yes, what you say."

"Let me pay for it," he said.

"No. I pay. No big money. You pay *beaucoup* money for rich American. I pay only 4,000 *dong*. You stay with me tonight?" she asked.

"Yes, I'll stay with you every night if you say it's OK."

"That be OK. I like."

"Is it safe for me to stay here?" he asked her.

"No VC here. I know about VC, I tell you."

The next morning, and after little rest, Clint walked back to the compound.

He felt very good until he saw Rossitor waiting for him. "Where were you last night?"

"I was at my girlfriend's house."

"In know," Rossitor said. "Where did you meet her?"

"In Vung Tau."

"She's probably a spy, Lieutenant McGregor."

"She is not. She doesn't care about the military. If she starts asking too many questions, I'll dump her."

"I don't like this one bit," Rossitor said. "I want you to dump her now."

"I'm not going to do that," Clint responded, keeping his anger under control.

Agitated, Rossitor said, "This is going into my report. I hope you know you're ruining your military career. Furthermore, we can't protect you outside the compound at night."

"I'll take my chances."

CHAPTER 13

Expert in Counterinsurgency

Vung Tau, South Vietnam, 1970

Clint walked into the little duplex unit on the canal and said, "Lien, I have something to tell you. I have to go to training. I'll be back as soon as I can."

With an accusatory scowl on her face, Lien said, "You number ten me? You have girlfriend?"

Hoping to avoid another unreasonable jealous squabble, "No, no. I've told you I love you. I don't want anyone else. You need to trust me."

"*Troi oi!*"

"I have to go to extra training to make me a better soldier."

"I don't want better soldier." Then she hugged him around the waist. "I want you be with me."

"I don't want to go either." With his hand he gently pressed her head to his chest. "But I'll be back. You wait for me."

"I wait. How long? When you go?"

"I'll be gone about ten days but I don't know when I'll leave. I've been told to be ready to go at any time. It will be soon. Don't tell anyone I'm gone."

"Who I tell? I know no one here. Maybe I go ma, see babysaun. You leave, you come back quick," she said with a sad downcast resigning look. "I still be here."

That afternoon Clint got a radio message that a helicopter

would pick him up in ten minutes at the team house chopper pad. His duffle bag was already packed. It would be another speedy trip to Vung Tau for Phoenix Advisor training.

On the first day of class, the American civilian leader in the region, John Vann, who had CIA written all over him, told the assembled junior officers, "I'm very satisfied with the way things are going. Much of our success is due to the Phoenix Program. I'm satisfied because things are simply getting better for us and harder for the enemy. The enemy is losing strength – a third off deltawide in the last six months, despite the North Vietnamese. The Northerners are the question mark, of course. But if it goes on as it's been going, I'm ready to project that by the end of this year the guerrilla war will be largely over in the Delta. Maybe I ought to allow another four to six months. But if it goes on as it's been going, once again, I'm confident that the Delta will be the government's strongest base before 1971 is over."

Clint released an inadvertent quiet groan as Vann strutted out of the classroom. In the expected show of respect all the students stood at attention as he left the room.

Next, a major addressed the Phoenix Advisor class. "Mister Vann is a brilliant leader. I have a success story to relate to you. Who is here from Hau Nghia Province?"

A captain raised his hand.

The major smiled at him and said, "Hau Nghia is still one of the ten worst Viet Cong provinces."

His classmates pointed and hooted at him.

"OK, that's enough. Actually, I've got some good news. Hau Nghia's been largely untouched until one recent chain of events," the major continued. "When a high ranking VCI died in combat, papers on his body led to the arrest of seven other VCI. People of the district, feeling that Saigon for the first time had the upper hand, began turning in names of other VCI. This further raised the hopes to break the back of Viet Cong control. This is how the Phoenix Program should operate. Every body, every captive and every building may lead us to intelligence on other enemy leaders and a fostering of confidence among the people to help us win their freedom."

"They make it sound like we're winning the war," Clint mumbled.

The officer seated next to him scowled in his direction.

On this trip to Vung Tau, Clint got more rest at night than his last trip and paid attention in class.

Nine days later each student received a certificate, a handshake from a colonel, and acknowledgement as an "expert" in counterinsurgency.

Clint caught a short helicopter jaunt to Saigon, then waited three hours to board a flight to Can Tho where he stayed overnight at a comfortable CIA hotel. The next morning he went by helicopter to Long Xuyen. From there he boarded a ferry with about 300 Vietnamese to cross the river to Sa Dec province and then hitched a Jeep ride with a South Vietnamese officer to Lap Vo.

He felt like he was returning home.

To demonstrate his growing knowledge of the Vietnamese language, upon his arrival in Lap Vo, he told the Vietnamese officer *"Cam on* ('Thank you')."

The officer, evidently wanting to show off his English responded, "You are welcome."

Clint was not unhappy to learn Rossitor had been

transferred out while he was away. Although Clint valued the information Rossitor had imparted to him, he found his judgmental attitude irksome.

Sure enough, Lien was waiting for him. They did not waste any time stripping their clothes off and jumping into bed.

During the next week Captain Roy and Clint observed four village elections. All four villages responded with a high voter turnout. The method of voting was unique, Clint thought. Each elector was handed a little stack of printed papers. Each piece of paper had a candidate's name printed on it along with an identifying logo.

Voters selected the slip of paper for the candidate they favored and dropped it into the ballot box. The unused slips were tossed into a trash box. Clint wondered how many of the discarded ballots were later counted too.

"The ballot symbol each candidate uses to identify themselves is real interesting," Clint said to Roy. "Look at these. Here is a ballot logo with a line drawing of an umbrella, a symbol of protection. And here's one with a plow, which means hard work, I guess. And another with a peasant working in a rice paddy, for the 'everyman' candidate. My favorite is the one with the picture of a man standing with his family. How could you vote against your family?"

"That family only has three children," Roy said. "That's not very typical."

"Well, maybe he's in favor of birth control too."

"I doubt it."

"Even though unsophisticated, these little pictures say a lot," Clint said. "Some people are just natural politicians."

"In my neighborhood, the politicians give out 'wakin'

around' money," Roy said.

"That sounds like bribery."

"Naw, we consider it travel expenses."

A few days later Clint visited an American Mobile Advisory Team in My An Hung Village. He was surprised to see that they lived no better than the South Vietnamese Popular Forces. Their fort was packed mud, concertina wire, and cleared fields of fire guarded with Claymore mines. This outpost of seven American soldiers was the only other U.S. installation in the district. They invited Clint to stay the night but he declined the opportunity to sleep with rats, spiders and snakes. Instead he hired a motor scooter to take him back to Lien before nightfall.

The rainy season began early. It rained ever day at 3:30 in the afternoon, which lowered the temperature and increased the humidity. It rained so hard at times that helicopters were grounded, water leaked through brick and mortar walls, and confused fish swam up on land. The weather reminded Clint of driving through a car wash.

The Vietnamese, always ready to conform to what nature had to offer, ran outside with bars of soap and washed themselves, and the minimal clothes they were wearing, in the downpours.

CHAPTER 14

"Congressional pigs"

<u>Long Hung Village, South Vietnam, 1970</u>

An hour after the downpour began, it diminished to a drizzle; then a clear sky seared the wetness off any solid object. The bathers dried themselves with the help of the sun and the disoriented fish flopped back into the canals. Everywhere steam made breathing a chore. The temperature of the misty air rose rapidly. The welcome coolness the rain temporarily brought was quickly forgotten.

Clint sidestepped the remaining puddles as he ambled to the duplex unit he shared with Lien. He may have looked nonchalant as he walked but he had become alert to all his surroundings. Clint would not have admitted it but the Phoenix Advisor training program and the constant alerts to danger had changed him. Lien and Clint's teammates noticed it. He was harder, more determined, smiled less. The mischievous glint in his eye had subsided. He would not talk about the training he had gone through. Even though he still expressed cynical attitudes, he took his job more seriously. He was tense and constantly armed. No longer did he go outdoors without his flack jacket. Hours were spent reading secret documents, drawing charts depicting the VC chain-of-command in his area, and talking quietly with his counterpart, Captain Chuong.

With Lien, however, he was still gentle, understanding, and patient.

Lien was already preparing the evening meal when he arrived, soaked from unevaporated perspiration. The air felt like wet cotton candy. As soon as he got inside the door, he stripped off his clothes down to his loose fitting boxer shorts.

Lien brought him a damp cloth for his brow and the rest of his body. She handed him a tall glass of tea and apologized that she had no ice. She told him to lie in the mesh hammock where the air circulation would cool him. Since there were no windows in the hooch, she opened both the front and back doors to allow for air circulation. When she tied back the plastic curtain that separated the front from the back of the cabin, a gentle breeze passed through the small dwelling.

Before he headed to the net hammock, he kissed her on the lips and patted her round bottom. She giggled and pushed him away. From the gradually swinging hammock he continued to watch and admire her as she chopped and poured and sprinkled various substances unknown to him into a metal pot. Dressed in a short cotton nightgown, and with nothing worn underneath, she looked cool, efficient and confident. Clint watched her work and was occasionally rewarded with a brief glimpse of breast or thigh and hair falling into her face, oblivious to his fascination.

Clint had more on his mind these days because expectations of him were increasing. He thought about his mounting correspondence and record keeping; about the untrustworthy Vietnamese woman who was appointed his secretary to type his messages into her native language; about his worthless interpreter who was said to be sick and would be gone for a month.

He gazed at the little temple Lien had created inside their apartment with a small Buddha and tin cans filled with sand to hold incense sticks. In the evening, after dinner, she would light the sticks and wave some of the smoke toward themselves. Clint took an interest in the Hoa Hoi sect of the Buddhist religion and began wearing a little Buddha on a chain around his neck. The villagers appreciated his respect for their religion.

With his head elevated, while lying in the hammock, Clint gulped the tea from the tall glass. He had no appetite because of the heat but hoped he would be hungry by the time Lien was done cooking. He did not want to disappoint her.

Suddenly Lien stepped into the front room and handed Clint a hand fan with which to cool himself. He fanned himself for a while and then began to doze.

Clint was suddenly awakened by Lien saying, "We eat now."

Clint rolled out of the hammock and joined her near the open backdoor where they ate with both chop sticks and a table spoon. The salty noodle soup with rice, chunks of vegetables, and shrimp was tasty. They also consumed French bread, which they dipped into the hot soup. They shared a can of Coca-Cola Clint brought from the team house.

While Clint sat on the floor with his legs crossed, Lien squatted flat footed while they ate. Clint knew she could probably squat this way for hours without her legs getting tired. When he tried sitting like this, he felt awkward and his legs began the scream for mercy after about five minutes. He assumed the Vietnamese learned to sit this way because they often had no chairs to sit on. Also, he observed that Vietnamese were slimmer and more flexible than Americans.

"Lien, this food is good."

"I happy you like."

"You take good care of me."

"We both take care of other," she said.

"What did you do today?" he asked, just to make conversation.

"I go to market early. Go early, find best food. Go late, all good food gone. Only lazy, not good woman, go late. Remember, I go before you wake up? You try to make me stay in bed."

"Yes, I remember," he said with a chuckle.

"I like stay in bed, but sometime I can't. We go bed early tonight. That be OK?"

"Definitely OK."

"We go bed after I wash dishes and pray Buddha."

An hour later they were in bed together and the doors were locked shut. They lay on a white sheet; he was still wearing boxer shorts and she in her short nightgown. The stillness and heat inside their hooch was oppressive. Mosquito netting protected them from flying insects, but further deadened air circulation.

"You look good," she said in the fading light.

"You're beautiful and kind and smart. How did I get so lucky?

"Yes, you very lucky man," she teased.

He rolled toward her and kissed her in the middle of her laugh.

"You taste like *nounc mam*," she said.

"<u>You</u> taste like *nounc mam*," he responded.

"We both fishy?"

"Yes, I think so."

"Too bad, you no like fish," she said.

"Oh, I love fish," he said.

"Did you catch me in a net?"

"I thought you caught <u>me</u>."

"Maybe catch each other," she said.

Clint reach under her nightshirt, exposing the bottom half of her slim body, felt the smooth skin on her lower back, and pulled her close.

"Honey, you hot, you sweat," she said.

"Aren't you hot?"

"Yes, I hot. Maybe too hot to boom-boom. Maybe make love in morning."

"Don't you have to go to the market?"

"I go *ti ti* late."

"What did you say about women who go to the market late?"

"I be bad woman to be good to you."

"I have to go early too. I'm going to Long Hung Village, by myself unfortunately, to meet the President's inspection team."

"You no tell me that! No tell me what you do."

"Why?"

"What if VC catch me? Make me talk. I tell something about you. You be dead."

"You're right; you're right. I won't say anything about what I'm doing. I don't want anything to endanger us."

"You think before you talk."

"It's just that I trust you."

"OK . . . you go sleep now."

A half hour later, Clint was not asleep. He heard a dog bark in the distance. A mosquito or maybe ten buzzed in the air outside the netting. Some water splashed, probably someone dumping garbage into the canal.

"Lien?"

"What you want?"

"It's too hot to sleep."

"I help you sleep."

"How?"

"I fan you, so you sleep."

"What? I can't ask you to do that!"

"You no ask. I do."

"But you won't be sleeping if you do that."

"That be OK. I sleep later."

She began fanning him with a cardboard fan shaped like a leaf. *How unselfish,* he thought. He began to feel more comfortable, drowsy, and was soon sound asleep.

He awoke early with the crowing of a rooster. Upon opening his eyes in the dim light he saw Lien sitting beside him, the fan still in her hand and her eyes closed. She had fallen asleep sitting up. He gently lowered her to their bed, took the fan from her hand, and kissed her forehead.

He dressed quietly and walked to the compound to take a shower. When he got to the gate he found the guards asleep. He yelled at them and they jumped to their feet, smiled, bowed, and saluted.

Upon entering the lounge in the team house Binh informed Clint that his interpreter's father was killed by the VC. He could not help think that even though the father could buy his son a non-combat position, it also made him a target for elimination by the VC.

Then Binh told him that the shaggy black dog had run away. Clint had a strange feeling that both the translator and the dog had arrived together; then disappeared together. He wondered if he would ever see the two of them again.

He did not have time to worry about either of them at the moment. He had to make preparations to drive the Jeep to Long Hung Village. He rustled through some newspapers and military reports to update himself on the visitation by President Nixon's delegation.

Nixon had formed a "fact finding committee" of congressmen, governors, and White House staffers to tour South Vietnam and Cambodia, including one of Clint's villages. Senator William Fulbright of Arkansas and Senator Frank Church of Idaho called the tour a public relations ploy. Herbert Klein, Nixon's director of communications, said the mission was "certainly not" a propaganda effort. Bryce Harlow, counselor to the president, said the delegation would "report exactly what they see and what they hear with total objectivity."

Clint figured his area was selected for a visit because no one was likely to get shot there during the day and the villagers would be compliant. The reception they would receive was certain to be positive and well orchestrated.

Clint had been told he was welcome to attend the briefing the VIP's would receive. He was also instructed not to wear his flack jacket or carry a rifle since this was a "pacified" village. So, he would conceal Colonel Hu's corroded little pistol under his shirt.

Clint knew that even though the village was "friendly," it was rife with corruption, just like most of South Vietnam's government. Somehow he wanted to inform the visiting civilians of this fact.

He drove the team Jeep as fast as the rutted road would permit and arrived in the village at the appointed time for the visitation. Local civilian and military leaders stood in the village square ready to greet the fact finding committee. The day was sunny and the temperature was tolerable for a change, so waiting for the delegation was not uncomfortable.

Two hours behind schedule three shiny helicopters swooped over the village, circled it, then one-by-one landed in a nearby field, raising a cloud of dust. Out of the 'copters bounded politicians with cameras hanging from their necks, presidential staffers with notebooks at the ready, and a small cluster of strutting generals.

As they approached the village market, thumping drums greeted them, Vietnamese soldiers stood at attention, and police and military officers saluted. On cue the villagers cheered just as they had practiced. On display was a paper dragon and young people dressed as dancing monkeys.

To the politicians it looked like a campaign, so they waved to the small crowd and shook hands with surprised bystanders. Governor Raymond Shafer of Pennsylvania looked like he was running for district chief. Evidently no one told him it was an appointed position.

The delegation, with happy smiles on their faces, made their way toward the two room village headquarters. They walked up the main street that had been graded and graveled the day before.

Keeping pace with the visitors was Lieutenant Clint McGregor. He recognized Governor Robert McNair of

South Carolina, said to be one of the new breed of moderate Southern Democrats.

"Governor, I'd like to show you some misuse of foreign aid," Clint said. The governor did not turn his head or acknowledge the comment.

"This school house we're passing on our left is so unsafe parents won't send their children there. Most of the cement was stolen before it arrived here. So, to make up for it, too much sand was added to the cement mix. And there's no back wall to this building because the bricks were stolen. It looks like a nice stucco school building from the front, but if you look at the back of it with me, you'll see that it's open. It's safe enough for pigs but not for kids . . ." McNair ignored him and kept on walking.

A little further down the road the delegation was shown the "pig cooperative." A little corral had been built and stocked with some very clean looking pigs. Clint was surprised because he had never noticed the pig pen before.

Once inside the crowded village headquarters, a CIA agent was given ten minutes to explain the "pacification" of Long Hung Village. The agent began by orientating them to their location, the history of the village, and the meaning of pacification. When he began to say something about the inefficiency (a code word for "dishonesty") of the local leaders and the delegation began to ask questions, John Vann stepped forward to remind them that they were behind schedule and lunch would be waiting at their next stop. Vann wrapped things up with a little speech about the growing feeling of nationalism among the South Vietnamese people.

The delegation was whisked away, waving and smiling at

the crowd while the local leaders waved and smiled back. In another cloud of dust, the fact finders were gone, having captured some good photos in their cameras.

Once the helicopters were out of sight, the villagers stopped by the government pig pen to retrieve their recently washed pigs and took them home. Among American advisors, the healthy looking animals became known as the "Congressional pigs."

CHAPTER 15

Willing participants

Lap Vo, South Vietnam, 1970

Colonel Hu hosted another party at his impressive estate. And as before, Clint noticed the local warlord was late to his own gathering so he could get a standing ovation when he entered with a dignified wave and a big smile on his round face. Captain Chuong and Lieutenant Clint McGregor, seated next to each other, rose to their feet and applauded along with everyone else.

The cognac flowed freely and Chuong and Clint were willing participants in the mid-year festivities. Young women, all wearing matching white *ao dai* made sure their glasses were always filled.

The traditional *ao dai* is a tight-fitting silk tunic worn over pantaloons. Clint admired Vietnamese women for knowing the secret of being very sexy while completely covered.

"Why are we celebrating?" Clint asked Chuong.

"This is the mid-year party."

"Why are we celebrating the middle of the year?"

Chuong looked at him with a little expression of disdain. "We are celebrating because there are no other holidays in June. We are celebrating because we have survived another six months. We are celebrating because Colonel Hu said we would."

Clint failed to see the logic in that unexpectedly long explanation. "How many of these have you been to?"

"This is my third one. The first one I came to, I was only a lieutenant," he smirked

"Oh."

"Here comes the food," Chuong said.

"I'm ready."

Each person was given a bowl of a light soup with a little rice in it. This was followed by big platters of sticky rice, something that appeared to be fowl prepared in a variety of styles, pork with the skin and fat still attached, and onions and cucumbers seasoned with ample amounts of *nuoc mam*.

"Duck is traditional at mid-year parties," Chuong said.

"Is that what that is? It looks great," Clint responded enthusiastically.

The noise in the large paneled room quieted as chopsticks competed for the best pieces of duck. By now Clint was quite adept at using chopsticks but he could never get over the custom of using them to grab something off someone else's plate if it looked good. Clint learned quickly to eat the most desirable morsels first before losing them to someone with competing chopsticks sitting close by.

The bones and any other unwanted piece of food were thrown under the table to marauding dogs. The mongrels seemed to be in a party mood too.

The main course was followed by more drinking. The beverage of choice shifted to rice alcohol — that strong drink no one wanted to touch their lips. It was served in shot glasses and the clear liquid was thrown directly to the back of the throat and swallowed. Since it was not Clint's first experience with the concoction, he knew what to do.

Several inebriated old men struggled to their feet with the help of canes and the man seated next to them to toast Colonel Hu and the Republic of Vietnam. Chuong said the aged gentlemen were retired military officers who had fought with the French.

Clint noticed that the walls of Hu's banquet room were adorned with a huge yellow and red striped national flag and pictures of many famous world leaders, both past and present. There was a very large picture of Colonel Hu too. The portraits of Nguyen Van Thieu, the President of South Vietnam and Tran Thien Khiem, the Prime Minister, were conspicuous by their absence.

By the time Clint got back to the team house he was pretty wasted. Not much work was going to get done the rest of the day. Nevertheless, an "urgent message" was received from Military Assistance Command Vietnam saying that the VCI estimate was too high. All of the Phoenix Advisors in the IV Corps received the same notice. They were ordered to file a mid-May report "correcting errors" in last month's figures.

Ironically, Clint knew that Chuong was getting complaints from his superiors that his VCI count was too low. Clint understood that the Americans wanted low figures in order to demonstrate they were winning the war. The South Vietnamese officials wanted the figures to be higher in order to justify increased American assistance.

A couple weeks later Phoenix Advisors received a message from Wilbur Wilson, Assistant Deputy for Pacification, which stated, "The effort to refine the IV Corps estimate of the strength of the Viet Cong Infrastructure in the Delta have resulted in an initial 24% reduction. The total identified and estimated VCI, as reported through PHOENIX channels, is now 25,866 – down from the March figure of 33,320. While the desired goal was refinement, it is nonetheless satisfying to note that this commendable intelligence effort has also resulted in a lower number."

On the other side of the compound Captain Chuong was filing a new report to increase the number of identified VCI.

Later, Chuong and Clint compared their reports over a beer and both had a good laugh. Chuong told Clint, "I suggest you criticize me and I will criticize you and we will both get promoted."

That evening Lien and Clint took a sampan across the river to Binh Tam Trung village to see a Hoa Hao celebration. It was a three-day festival honoring their prophet's birthday.

After taking some pictures of the dragon dance with a flash camera, Clint began to feel uneasiness in his stomach. A trickle of sweat rolled down the side of his face. The flashing lights, the exploding firecrackers, the pushing of the crowd made him concerned for their safety. He had learned to trust his instincts.

He grabbed Lien's hand and bent down to quietly speak into her ear. "It's unsafe here. We must leave."

She looked up at him with her big brown eyes. "We go now," and she led him to the dock to hire a boat to cross the river to Lap Vo.

The next day Clint learned that a bomb exploded at the celebration, killing 12 and injuring 23. The Hoa Hao hated the communists and the feeling was mutual.

The following day Clint traveled to the nearby Vam Cong village where he met the District Police Advisor and two of his aides for lunch. They ate rice, huge Rach Gia shrimp, and pork. It was all washed down with beer, cold only because each glass had a big hunk of ice in it; probably frozen polluted water.

When the bill came Clint glanced at it, seeing the price came to 1700 *dong*. That was probably twice as much as a Vietnamese would have paid. He rose to complain about the cost but the police advisor grabbed his forearm and said, "That's OK. I've got it."

"I hate to be taken advantage of," Clint said.

"That's OK Lieutenant. Don't cause a fuss. It happens all the time."

When Clint got back to the team house that afternoon he sat down to drink another beer. Then he got a message over the team house radio. It was from a helicopter pilot who was flying over his district.

The pilot gave Clint the coordinates of their location and said, "I see two men running for cover. Should I engage them?"

Clint looked at his big map on the wall. The location was a large flat area that was once a rice paddy, now known as "The Triangle." It was a site where canals formed a perfect triangle on the map and was a hotbed of VC activity.

Clint responded, "You are over a free fire zone. No friendlies live in the area. You are authorized to take offensive action."

"You want me to eliminate them?"

"That's affirmative."

"Roger. Out"

There was silence on the radio for over a minute. Then the pilot came back on the radio. "There are now two less people living in The Triangle."

"Thank you. Good work."

CHAPTER 16
"Poor, dumb and scared"

The building looked like it could have been important once. Now it was just drab with dirt in the corners, squeaking ceiling fans in nearly every room, peeling cream colored paint inside and out, and geckos chasing each other on the walls.

Clint and Sergeant Binh, the interpreter, were seated in a room completely devoid of artwork, photos, or anything; except for a cheap folding table and three unstable folding chairs. Dusty shades covered the dirty windows. Hanging bare light bulbs provided the dim illumination in the room.

They sat next to each other at the table and the remaining chair, presently unoccupied, faced them from the other side of the table.

Clint, who was promoted to captain the day before in a little ceremony in Can Tho, looked over a briefing sheet in preparation to interview the three _hoi chanhs. Hoi chanhs_ were members of the Viet Cong who voluntarily surrendered to the government in exchange for employment training. They were also paid for any weapons they brought with them when they surrendered.

Clint was assigned by his superiors to interview the three in the hope he could obtain useful information from them. He did not know why he was suddenly given this assignment in Can Tho and he felt totally unprepared. The three to be interviewed were all low level functionaries in the VC, not likely to know anything about strategy or how decisions were made. He figured this was just part of the process for them to "rally" to the RVN side. Clint, still somewhat of an idealist, hoped they surrendered for ideological or political motives.

One was said to be a guerrilla fighter, another a medical aide, and the last a girl responsible for hamlet supply.

"I don't smoke, so I guess I can't give them cigarette burns to get them to talk."

Binh, always wanting to be helpful, said, "Sir, I bet I can get you some electrical wires around here to give them shocks."

"Binh, I was just kidding. I'm not going to mistreat them. They are on our side now."

"Yes, but we should not trust them. They are going to be scared shitless anyway. You have the power to send them to the classroom or to jail."

"Shitless? Shitless? Binh, that's a new word for you," Clint said with a chuckle.

"Yes, sir," Binh said with mock seriousness. "I'm expanding my English vocabulary every day."

"OK. Good. Let's get started."

"They should be just outside the door."

"Bring the guerrilla fighter in first."

A short stocky young man came into the room and took the seat across from the table and gave his name as directed.

"Where did you operate and where did you rally to our side?" Clint asked.

"I operated in Phong Dinh province and I rallied in Can Tho," Binh translated.

"Who was your commanding officer?"

"I don't know," he said. "The fighters I was with were all equal."

Clint expected he was withholding information. "Why did you join the VC?

"I was forced to work for the VC. They said they would harm my family if I did not fight with them."

"What was your job with the VC?"

"My job was to lay booby-traps with two other men. I only knew these two men and our platoon leader. I did not know anyone else." Clint noticed the contradiction; first the young man said all in his unit were equal, but just now he mentioned his platoon leader.

"What is the platoon leader's name?"

He promptly answered the question.

Binh interjected, "Captain, he gave a name that is very common. Having that name is not helpful to us."

"Write it down anyway," Clint told the interpreter. "Where is he now?" he asked the young man across the table from him.

"He was killed."

"Do you believe in communism?" Clint continued.

Binh said, "He does not understand the question."

Clint said, "Ask him if he was fighting for a cause"

In response to the question, he said, "I wanted to protect my family."

"Yes, we heard that before," Clint said. "Can you read?"

"Yes. I went to school when I was young."

"Do you read propaganda leaflets?"

"Yes. That is how I know about this training program for those who leave the VC."

"What kind of training do you want?"

"I want to be a farmer."

"OK," Clint said. "It was nice to meet you. And I hope you become a farmer and not have to fight anymore."

The ex-guerrilla fighter stood, bowed slightly and put his hands together as if in prayer. "May I go to class now?"

"Yes, that is all for today," Binh told him in Vietnamese.

Clint said, "Send in the medic next."

The medic quietly appeared and took a seat at Binh's direction.

"Why did you join the VC?" Clint asked.

"I joined because I thought it would be fun and exciting."

"Was that the only reason?"

"Yes."

"Didn't you want to change the government too?" Clint asked

The former medic thought for a moment. "I don't know anything about the government. I wanted to get a rifle."

"Why did you leave the VC?"

"It is very dangerous. My friends were killed. And I did not get a rifle. If somebody shot at me I could not shoot back."

"What unit were you with?"

"I don't know about units. I worked like a nurse. I was at an aid station with three other men. They brought the sick and wounded to us. We never went to the unit. I never shot anyone. But I saw a lot of people who were shot."

"Do you know your village and hamlet chief?" Clint asked.

"No. I do not know them."

"Do you know what communism is?"

"No. I do not."

"What kind of training do you want?"

"I want to learn how to read."

"Didn't you go to school?"

"I went to school sometimes but it got blown up and mothers were afraid to send their children to school."

"Will you go back to the VC?"

"No."

"That is all. I hope you learn to read. Send in the next person," Clint said.

The former medic left with a big smile on his face. He looked relieved.

The girl walked in very shy with her head down.

After she sat, Clint asked, "How old are you?"

"Fifteen."

"Why did you join the VC?"

"I grew up VC because my parents are VC and my village is VC. I did not know it was wrong," she said, near tears. "I am sorry for what I did."

"How did you help the VC?"

"I collected rice from certain houses and gave it to a woman."

"Did you do anything else for the VC?"

"No."

"She's lying," Binh told Clint in English.

"We know you did other things for the VC. What were they?"

"Sometimes I collected taxes too. And I told people about meetings."

"What kind of training do you want?"

"I want to be a seamstress and make clothes. When I make

clothes I will make money and I will save some money so someday I can buy a Singer sewing machine."

"Where do your parents live?"

"Long way from here. They live in Phuoc Long province."

"Do you know what 'communism' is?"

"I do not know."

"Why did you surrender?"

"Because the VC is becoming weak and the RVN is getting stronger. If the war ever ends I want to be on the winning side."

"I hope you learn how to sew and not help the VC anymore."

"I hope so too," she said with a nervous smile.

After she left the room, Clint said, "All three were the bottom of the food chain for the VC. They did not know anything. They sounded like they did not even know what they were fighting for."

"And if they did, they weren't going to tell us," Binh said. "They are all poor, dumb, and scared."

"I'm not going to give people who say they want to be on our side a hard time. This is their second chance. They'll be watched closely. If they screw up again the consequences will be fatal."

Binh said, "Yes. If we can catch them."

"When we get back to Lap Vo I will write up my report," Clint said. "Right now I think it's time for a beer."

The chairs scraped on the gritty tile floor as they pushed back from the table.

CHAPTER 17

"You stole too much"

Lap Vo, in fact most of the Vietnam Delta, was deceptively peaceful. People smiled, little streams meandered, slow moving canals accommodated quaint looking sampans, and the sunny humidity begged people to take it easy. The laughing children at play were the only ones in a hurry.

The peasants knew they would always be peasants, and so would their many children. Parents believed it important for their kids learn to read, write, and do simple math. There was no need for further education. Nevertheless, the Vietnamese had a high literacy rate and were justifiably proud of it.

While most Vietnamese were not materialistic, a few were. They tended to be military officers, politicians, and policemen. Businessmen adept at smuggling could also be added to their number. Graft was a means to advancement. As long as it was subtle, quiet, and not extreme, it was tolerated. The line between acceptable and extreme graft was a thin one. The higher one's status, the more graft they were obliged to take.

It was OK to expect a kickback for employing someone in a safe job. For many it was acceptable to take a small amount of material from a construction site. It was normal to pay "taxes" to policemen in cash with no questions asked and no records kept.

With Lien visiting her son and mother in An Giang, Clint opted for sleeping in his bedroom at the team house. He awoke expecting an ordinary humid, hot, and slow day. He lay under the mosquito netting. The huge domesticated pig outside his open air window began to grunt and stir up unpleasant smells. Roosters commenced to crow, as Vietnamese soldiers lay on their bunks smoking while waiting for reveille, and as women cooked noodle soup for breakfast. Little sampans with one or two people in them fished in the river as the sun broke over the green horizon. The market on the main street was coming alive. It was morning in Lap Vo.

Even though it was early, two white shirted policemen were heard knocking at the front door of the team house. Sergeant Binh, already on the job, jumped to answer it. The pair of cops, more inclined to kick doors down, strained to be respectful at the American outpost.

Clint, who was learning a little Vietnamese with Lien's help, heard something about returning the Jeep. He slipped on some trousers and sandals and came to the door bare-chested. Clint saw the Jeep parked by the front door, in its usual place, just as he left it.

"Binh, what's the problem?"

"Just a minute, sir. Let me get the whole story."

Binh listened to the policemen. He responded a couple times to what they were saying. Then he dismissed them. They bowed and left.

Impatiently, Clint asked, "What's up?"

"Yes, sir. Good morning. Your 18-year-old translator hit someone with the Jeep. But it's OK. The man was not hurt very bad and Colonel Hu paid the fine for the young man."

"Colonel Hu? Oh, shit. But I didn't know Phuc was back from sick leave and I didn't loan him the Jeep; he must've just taken it."

"Colonel Hu not only paid the fine, but also gave money to the injured man. I'm sure he also paid some taxes to each of the policemen. There will be no report. Everything is settled."

"The hell it is. Wait 'til I get a hold of that malingering draft dodging punk."

Graft and favors go together. Now we owe the local war lord a favor that he may want to collect on at any time, Clint thought.

Clint's morning rest was over. He wondered how long it would take for the interpreter to have guts enough to show up for work.

Next, Captain Chuong came to the team house to inform Clint that two roadside bombs had already killed three people that morning. The main road between Lap Vo and Sa Dec was closed at night and theoretically opened early every morning after having been inspected for mines laid by the VC overnight.

"How was the mine clearing conducted this morning?" Clint asked.

Without emotion Chuong said, "By someone announcing, 'The road is now open!'"

Clint could not figure out whether this was a serious answer or not. But he had gotten the same answer to a similar question previously. Evidently it was true. Clint felt like lecturing someone about mine reconnaissance and removal but he knew it would do no good.

Then Chuong reported on last night's military operation. "The clearing operation in The Triangle did not achieve the desired results. Most of the casualties came from South

Vietnamese soldiers stepping on land mines in the dark. Nine of our soldiers were killed, eight wounded, and six civilians were also injured. Evidently, the Viet Cong fled the area to avoid direct contact with us. That can be interpreted as progress."

Captain Chuong is sounding more like a bureaucrat every day, Clint thought. *The fact that he did not report enemy casualties meant the operation went very badly.*

Clint's frustrating day was just beginning. His report for the month of June had listed seven VC killed. Higher command had informed both Chuong and Clint that the "quota" was eight kills in the district for the month. Meeting the quota would have resulted in awards of 5,000 *dong* for Vietnamese officers and noncommissioned officers.

Chuong said, "Forgive me for saying this. Americans say, 'Tell it like it is;' Vietnamese say this is rude. But since you like rude I will tell you. My sergeants are complaining about you. You cost them money and they do not have lots of money."

"There were seven killed. Not eight. I can't lie to my superiors in my report. They're beginning to ask for evidence for each kill I report. Too many times when someone is killed they're called VC, when they're not. And then their name is held in dishonor and their widow gets no money."

"My friend, since you are a captain now you can be my friend; it is easy to find one more kill for your report. We can easily shoot a prisoner who tries to escape or a suspect who will not cooperate. My men say you are selfish and you do not care about them."

"That's not true."

"But they have worse to say about you."

"What's that?"

"They say you are a weak leader."

Clint scowled.

"I am sorry to tell you these things. You Americans want honesty. Too much honesty can be a bad thing. It can make people unhappy. It is better to be happy."

"Chuong," Clint smiled, "Now that we're equal rank, I can say this. You're so full of shit."

"Ok, you say that now. Now I have some shit to give you."

"I can't wait. What now?"

"Did you see that barge at the village dock?"

"How could I miss it?"

"The barge is hauling bricks, cement, sand, and lumber and it stopped at our little canal port of Lap Vo. You are asked to certify that all the supplies have reached Lap Vo and it is approved to go upstream to the next district where construction is taking place."

"What am I supposed to do? Count all the bricks and weigh the sand? It doesn't look like a full barge load to me. What happens if I refuse to sign?" he asked Chuong.

"Then the barge will stay here to block the port and the construction upstream will have to stop."

"Oh, great. Do you think it's all there?" Clint asked.

"Of course not. Each village chief charged a small tax in order to let the barge go by their village. The tax was paid with building materials from the barge," Chuong said.

"Was it a tax or a bribe?"

Chuong looked peeved. "You Americans are so picky."

Clint hesitated.

"You see, the district chief has already signed." Chuong pointed to the chief's signature on the document. "He gave it to me for you to sign too."

Clint grabbed the paper and scribbled his name. "Here's my damn signature."

Clint knew the unauthorized off-loading of a few supplies at each village was a minor offense compared to the graft he read about at higher levels. He hated being a part of the barge materials scam but refusing to sign could result in dire consequences. Not signing would mean the huge barge would block the Lap Vo dock from doing any further business. The construction upstream would have come to a halt too. And since the district chief had already signed, refusing to add his name would be like calling the chief a liar. The chief could easily withdraw the security his troops provided Clint and his teammates. With so much disruption, Clint could easily be labeled a troublemaker by his superiors and sent to a more dangerous post as punishment.

One benefit of being an intelligence officer, Clint often acquired information that the average soldier or civilians would never see. A secret government report he received recently rumored the new District Police Chief paid 50,000 *dong* for his job. He could quickly recoup his investment, however. His police squad was required to pay him 10,000 *dong* a day. The police officers obtained this money by setting up highway checkpoints to allegedly catch VC. The "taxes" they collected at the roadblocks were on an "ability to pay" basis. If someone refused to pay, however, they were arrested as a VC suspect. Every Vietnamese paid. Bus traffic was particularly lucrative.

The District Police Chief did not keep all the money his policemen collected. He was required to send 30,000 *dong* a month to the Province Police Chief.

Another secret report alleged the Sa Dec and Chau Duc province chiefs had a means to supplement their incomes. The Sa Dec chief agreed to buy all their rock and gravel from Chau Duc Province at exorbitant prices; the profit was then divided by the two province chiefs. The transportation of this rock and gravel was free-of-charge, courtesy of the United States. It was hauled in U.S. Army trucks with U.S. Army drivers.

Clint wondered why U.S. officials did nothing about this graft if they knew so much about it. *Probably efforts to stop it got very complicated very fast. Just like me not doing anything about the barge traffic graft that goes right through my district. Maybe sending this information out is a plea for help. They can't stop it but hope that if enough people are informed, someone will do something.*

Clint soon learned that Major Angelo was getting increasingly fed up with the level of corruption he observed. "Hey, Clint. Want to see something entertaining? I'm going to haul in that crook from Hoi An Dong village and rake him over the coals."

"Maybe I can learn something from my superior officer."

"We'll see. Binh, please inform the outgoing village chief at Hoi An Dong that I want to see him right away."

"Yes, sir." Binh jumped on his scooter and sped away.

A couple hours later the village chief appeared with a big friendly smile on his face. The Americans nicknamed him "Smiley" because he always had a smile on his face and his real name was too hard to pronounce.

Binh interpreted, "Chief, have a seat here, please."

"Would you like to have a Coca-Cola?" Clint asked.

"Yes, I would. Thank you. It was a long hot trip but I came as soon as I could. What can I do for you, gentlemen?"

Major Angelo began, "Part of my job is to protect the American taxpayer. All the public works are paid for by Americans and our allies. The Vietnamese pay very low taxes."

"Yes, sir."

"Do you know why you didn't get reelected?"

"Yes. I represent the peasants and they could not come to vote because they were too busy working in their rice patties."

Clint knew this to be a lie. Every citizen of South Vietnam carried a voter identification card. It was stamped to show they voted at the last election. If they could not produce such a stamped identification card, they could be arrested as a VC suspect.

"I heard you did not get reelected because you stole from the people," Angelo said.

"Oh, no sir," Smiley said, still with a smile on his face. "Maybe some taxes, but that does not go to me. That money goes to the government."

"You were poor when you first got elected. Is that right?"

"Yes, and I am still poor."

"I see you're wearing new clothes today. You look very nice."

"Thank you, sir."

"I didn't see anybody else in your village with new clothes when I last visited."

Smiley did not respond.

"But what really concerns me is that million *dong* house you're building. That's not the house of a poor man."

Smiley's smile was fading.

"I know where you got the money to build your house. You sold the material for building the new bridges in your village.

But the bridges were built anyway but because of you they're very weak bridges. They're dangerous because they weren't built with the right material. The American people wanted to help the economy of your entire village, not just you. What do you have to say for yourself?"

"You're mistaken, sir."

"The hell I am!" Angelo yelled, getting red in the face. "You stole too much. You hurt your village more than the VC could. Do you know what we do with VC around here?"

Smiley glanced around the room but all he saw was scowling faces. "Yes, I know what you do with VC but I am not VC."

"If you were VC, I'd shoot you. You need to be punished," Angelo said, warming to his subject. "I'm told that your crime is punishable by two years in prison, which sounds fair to me."

"I will die in prison." He was not smiling anymore.

Angelo knew the unreliability of the Vietnamese court system. Smiley might be able to bribe his way out of prison. "You're a bad example of democracy. But the people are not dumb. They voted you out of office because you put your personal welfare above the interests of the public. Every time someone walks by your new house they're going to think, 'That's where a crook lives.' What do you say?"

Smiley just shook his head.

"I'm not going to send you to prison. I tell you what I'm going to do. That bridge coming into your market is poorly built. I'm going to make you stand under that bridge while I drive over it in my Jeep," Angelo said.

Two days later that was exactly what the major did. With Vietnamese soldiers pointing their rifles at the village chief to make sure he did not flee the scene, Angelo, wearing a helmet and flack jacket, slowly drove his Jeep over the bridge. A small crowd gathered on the banks to laugh and hiss and clap and throw dirt clods at the village chief.

The glassy-eyed fear on Smiley's face was replaced with a sigh of relief when the bridge did not collapse.

Clint believed the newly elected village chief would steal far less than Smiley. That was considered progress.

Back at the team house that afternoon, Clint said, "Major Angelo, that was quite a scene. Smiley standing there sweating and you driving slowly gripping the steering wheel. How'd you know the bridge would hold up?"

"At West Point we get some engineer training. I thought it would support a Jeep but not a truck. Make sure that bridge gets posted in English and Vietnamese 'No Trucks.' At least it will make a good footbridge."

"Yes, sir." Clint admired Angelo as a creative and unorthodox leader. "We've got a problem I've been meaning to mention to you."

"What now?"

"We're running out of gasoline and I can't get Sa Dec to deliver any. If we run out of gasoline our electricity will stop. Without electricity, the beer in the refrigerator will get warm. Nobody likes to drink warm beer."

"How long have you been requesting more gas?"

"Ten days."

"How often have you made this request?"

"Just about every day. We're now just operating the generator a few hours a day."

"Have they said when we could expect our next delivery?"

"No. In fact, they said we don't need any gas."

"That's ridiculous and unacceptable. You've tried everything?"

"Yes, sir."

"OK. I'll take care of it."

"What're you going to do?"

"I'll personally threaten to cut off all radio communication with the province headquarters until gasoline is delivered."

"Isn't that mutiny?"

"No. That's what they do in the navy."

"Then, is it desertion?"

"No. We're not going anywhere. They're deserting us."

"How's that getting us more gas?"

"Think about it. How'd you like to be the officer in Sa Dec and the commanding officer in Can Tho asks, 'How is everything going in Lap Vo.' He can't very well say, 'I don't know. They won't talk to me.'"

"I see what you mean."

"That's right. No communication means no control. And they have to have control."

To test Angelo's resolve Sa Dec headquarters sent several messages to Lap Vo but they got no acknowledgement and no response.

Three 55-gallon drums of gasoline arrived by truck the next day. The driver said he would be making delivers in the future on a weekly basis.

CHAPTER 18

"Making a run tonight"

Long Hung Village, South Vietnam, 1970

Captain Chuong had a worried look on his smooth tanned face.

"OK. What's going on?" Clint asked. "I can tell something's goin' down by the look on your face."

"The district chief just told me the nighttime curfew on Highway 8A to Sa Dec is being lifted for commercial vehicles."

"Don't they read our reports that we send them?" Clint asked.

"They also read their own propaganda. Now they believe it."

"We've been reporting that this is a 'pacified' district but that doesn't mean we control it," Clint said.

Chuong said, "This decision had to be made at the province level since it includes more than one district."

"They don't know what's goin' on out here. We're the daytime government and the VC is the nighttime government."

"Eight trucks are making a run tonight. One PF platoon is going with them."

"That's interesting. What're they hauling?"

"Watermelons."

"You're shitting me."

"I hear you say it: I shit you not."

Clint wiped some sweat from his brow.

"I think we should go with them," Chuong said. "If all goes well we will get some of the credit. If they need support, you and I have the ability to call for reinforcements."

"I can call in air support if needed. You have plenty of PF soldiers you can count on," Clint said.

"Yes."

"Maybe we can eat watermelon on the way to Sa Dec."

Chuong, serious as usual, ignored the comment. "They're leaving at 2100 hours."

"Is that American time or Vietnamese time?" Clint never seemed to get tired of asking this stupid question.

"What do you think?"

The convoy of trucks and drivers was ready to move at 9:00 p.m. but the platoon of soldiers was still assembling. The young platoon leader scowled and looked unhappy to see two officers taking up posts at the back of the first truck.

The exhaust belching trucks and the platoon of scraggly PF soldiers left Lap Vo at 9:30 p.m.

The first half of the trip was uneventful. Clint and Chuong grew tired of breathing diesel fumes but thankful they had not chosen to ride the last truck where they would be breathing both fumes and dust.

The rough road made for a jarring uncomfortable ride. It was also getting quite boring.

Chuong nudged Clint out of his stupor when the convoy crossed the boundary entering a dangerous section of Long Hung village. The area had recently seen some minor Viet Cong activity.

The cluster of roadside population evidently was observing

the 10:00 p.m. curfew. The community television was off and locked shut. Even the oil lamps in homes were snuffed. The place had the feel of a ghost town.

As they entered a clearing Chuong flipped off the safety on his M16 rifle. Clint took the clue and did the same.

The lead truck driver suddenly slammed on his breaks. Among skidding tires, honking horns, and swearing, the other drivers were forced to stop as quickly as possible.

Somebody yelled in Vietnamese, "Trees are across the road!"

Chuong looked around the side of the truck, and sure enough, three trees were lying across the road, stopping traffic.

"Get ready," Chuong said.

Then gun fire. Four guerrilla fighters raced to the trucks yelling they were collecting VC taxes from the drivers. Those remaining in the woods laid down gunfire to cover the men sprinting to the trucks.

The PF soldiers were caught completely off guard. They ran and cowered in the roadside ditches, firing their guns wildly into the air. Chuong and Clint leaped to the ground, slid underneath the first truck, took cover behind big tires, and aimed and fired their rifles in the direction of the gun flashes.

"It sounds like the VC has AK-47's. Thank God, no machine guns," Chuong yelled to Clint.

"And some old M1 American rifles."

"How do you know?"

"Hear that 'ping?' That's the sound after the last bullet in the eight-round clip is fired by an M1. That's the first rifle I trained on."

One of the drivers jumped down to the ground and dove into a ditch. The rest of the drivers stayed in their cabs. Some tried to drive away but found there was no room to turn the big rigs. Others, when confronted by gun wielding VC, hesitated to hand over money. One of the truck drivers had his brains splattered all over the inside of the cab when he refused to cooperate.

"You take the one on the left and I'll take the one on the right," Clint said.

Within two seconds two VC lay on the dirt road bleeding to death. The two remaining tax collectors sprinted back to the relative safety of their comrades in the woods.

Most of the PF soldiers had jumped into the ditch on the right side of the road. The VC was hidden in the jungle on the other side of the road and about a hundred meters back. Clint and Chuong were stuck in the middle under the lead truck. Neither force could see where to shoot but that did not discourage them from shooting anyway.

Clint asked Chuong, "Would you rather be shot by the enemy or by friendly fire?"

Chuong stopped to think about it.

"Don't stop firing. Think about it later." *Jesus Christ; no sense of humor*, Clint mumbled to himself

The sporadic gun fight continued for a half hour. Soon most of the tires on the trucks were punctured. Clint and Chuong continued firing into the jungle.

A brave radio operator finally scrambled up to Chuong wearing his radio pack. Chuong got on the horn and asked for reinforcements. In half an hour seven PF platoons converged on the area. The VC, with two killed and an estimated four wounded, ran away to fight another day. They failed to collect any taxes. Bullet-riddled watermelons leaked from the trucks.

The soldiers guarded the trucks from both sides of the road while repairs were being made. It was daylight before the heavy vehicles were ready to roll again.

I'm not going to tell Lien about this little fire fight, Clint thought. *It would just make her worried.*

With a smile Clint asked Chuong, "When we get to Sa Dec, do you think it'll be too early to get a drink?"

"No, it will not be too early at all."

CHAPTER 19

"Sometimes he stumbles."

Lap Vo, South Vietnam, 1970

Another day started out peacefully in Lap Vo, but suddenly changed. John Vann, the top civilian advisor in the Delta, swooped into the Lap Vo headquarters by helicopter unannounced, strutted into the team house, and demanded a briefing on the spot.

"I want your standard briefing and I want it now," Vann said with his hands on his hips.

Clint, Roy and Alonzo looked at each other wondering what was expected of them. Major Alonzo nodded at Clint to respond.

"Yes, sir," Clint said, stepping forward. "I'm Captain Clint McGregor, the Phoenix Advisor."

"I know who you are."

"I'm prepared to give you a summary of our monthly hamlet and village security report. I inspect each of our twelve villages on a monthly basis. I can also answer questions you may have related to specific VCI and intelligence reports."

"Very well, proceed."

Clint was able to paraphrase the monthly report but concerned his comments were too general to satisfy the U.S. civilian leader in the province. He expected some follow-up questions but none were forthcoming.

Vann turned to Captain Roy and Major Alonzo.

"Sir, we weren't expecting you," Major Alonzo said with a smile.

"That's obvious," Vann scowled.

"But we are happy to answer any of your questions."

Vann asked, "What's the price of pork in the market?"

Alonzo looked at Roy for an answer.

Captain Roy said, "Sir, the price has not changed recently."

"That's a bullshit answer. You don't know the answer. Prices have a lot to do with civil stability and if you don't know the answer then you aren't doing your job."

"I'll find out, sir, and report back."

"Major Alonzo, what is the number of hectares planted in IR-8 rice in this district?"

"I'm not prepared to answer that question."

"Do you know what IR-8 rice is?"

"No sir."

"I suggest you find out. You're responsible for foreign aid. This is fast growing disease resistant rice we are providing Vietnamese farmers.

"OK, let's make this easy. Let me see your Standardized Briefing Chart. Are you keeping it up to date?"

"Sir, I have never heard of a Standardized Briefing Chart," Alonzo said, looking nervous for the first time Clint could remember.

Then Vann got really upset with the team. "This has been very disappointing. You are treating your important assignment here like a vacation. Maybe you would be better suited to a combat position. I'll be talking to your commanding officers."

Vann, who had been called "brilliant" in the press, was

not having a good week. Before he left he admitted that other districts were just as unimpressive as Lap Vo. A junior officer, who was accompanying Vann, handed Major Alonzo a couple notebooks of reports. "Read these," he said.

As a parting shot Vann said the team was living in too much space and too much luxury. Then he stomped off to his helicopter and disappeared into the sky.

Clint was reminded of the few times he was allowed into Vann's walled compound in Can Tho where there were tall, neat and well dressed guards, electricity twenty-four hours per day, clean water, air conditioning, maid service, and a swimming pool with a bar. Lounging around the pool was a bevy of pretty Vietnamese women.

Clint had no respect for the self-important John Paul Vann. He had done some research on him and found that in 1963, Vann was a Lieutenant Colonel attached to the South Vietnamese 7th Infantry Division. He planned an attack on a Viet Cong force at Ap Bac. At his disposal were nineteen helicopters, thirteen armored personnel carriers, thirteen fighter bombers 1,400 South Vietnamese troops, and an unlimited supply of napalm. They were opposed by 350 Viet Cong. Within the first few minutes of the battle the helicopters were shot down. By the end of the battle the VC slipped away into the jungle with an estimated eighteen killed while the Saigon forces lost eighty plus another one hundred wounded; three American advisors were also killed. The outcome was a great morale boost for the VC who proved they could successfully challenged the government forces.

Soon afterward Vann "resigned" from the Army with a statutory rape charge hanging over his head. Considered a world authority on counterterrorism, Vann returned to Vietnam two years later to run the U.S. Agency for International Development in Hau Nghia Province, near the Cambodian border. His second in command, Doug Ramsey, was captured by the Communists, while Vann escaped. With favorable press coverage, Vann was promoted up the ranks in the AID.

Clint informed Roy and Alonzo of Vann's background as they toiled the rest of the day and part of the next crafting briefing charts. Once the charts were completed they were stowed behind the couch in the day room, never be seen by anyone again.

Clint learned from confidential reports he read later that day that Vann had a lot of disappointments on his mind, so it must have been easy for him to take his frustrations out on the scaled back local advisory teams. Within a period of two weeks an embarrassing street fight broke out between American and South Vietnamese soldiers in Sa Dec, an anti-American demonstration was staged in front of the Province Tactical Operations Center, and the VC took over Duc Ton village for a couple hours and executed 40 people. Every night the Long Hung village was harassed by about 20 VC.

Perceived instability resulted in an increased number of inspections by both Vietnamese and American officials. One village got tired of repetitious inspections by higher-ups and figured out a way to relieve themselves of this irritant. Whenever the South Vietnamese officials made arrangements to visit the village the local soldiers put on a fake firefight. Hearing all the gunfire, the inspectors would reschedule for another day.

Not all conflict, however, was generated by the war.

Sometimes turmoil was purely home grown.

Binh told Clint of an uproar that took place in Bihn Thanh Tay village when the Deputy for Village Security, with liquor on his breath, broke up a prayer meeting of Hoa Hao believers because they were violating the midnight curfew. "A few of the religious leaders were even put in jail for the night," Binh said. Villagers were incensed because some elderly ladies were prohibited from reading scripture. They argued that since there was no VC in their village, the curfew should not be upheld. No one had enforced the curfew in the past, they argued.

According to Binh, the security deputy countered in his own defense, "But no one had read the scriptures so loud and so late."

The dispute went on for days. "Finally, in order to resolve the issue, the village chief had the offending official's head shaved as punishment," Binh said.

"That sounds kind of primitive," Clint said.

"Maybe unusual but not unheard of. Anyway, that was not a strong enough punishment to satisfy some of the believers. They thought he should be locked in his own jail.

"The issue was still hot when the village chief held his monthly meeting with villagers. The village chief required his Deputy for Security to attend the meeting. The leading Hoa Hao believers tried to turn the meeting into a trial of the security official.

"Some stood and said the man who defiled their religion should be replaced. After many people had an opportunity to speak, the village chief said, the security official was 'right in action but not in temperament. He was carrying out his duty.'

"You can imagine this statement did not calm the crowd."

Clint could envision the security deputy, who he had met once, silently sitting in a corner in his black pajamas, his gold capped teeth covered with closed lips.

"Now here is the good part," Binh said, enjoying his story. "After more debate and bickering an elderly farmer struggled to his feet to speak. As a respected elder, the room became silent. He said, 'We are mostly religious people here. Our religion teaches us to forgive. We must learn to forgive those who go astray. A cow has four legs and she sometimes stumbles on the rocks. But man has only two legs, so sometimes he stumbles and falls. We are all men of two legs. We must learn to forgive our fellow man. It is part of the Hao Hoa religion.' The meeting concluded with no more argument. In the past that would have been the end of it. But maybe you Americans have taught us democracy too good. People who were upset decided to have a vote."

"You mean like a recall?" Clint asked.

"Yes, I guess that is what you call it," Binh said. "They voted to fire the Deputy for Security. He was kicked out of office."

"Then what happened?" Clint asked.

"Then the village chief, an honest and honorable man, resigned in protest."

That's democracy, Clint thought. *Sometimes people get the kind of government they deserve.*

CHAPTER 20

Three Frightened VC

Sa Dec Province, South Vietnam, 1970

When Clint prepared to leave their little house on the canal the next morning, Lien was fearful. She put her arms around him and said, "You no die. You die, I die."

"OK, I promise not to die today," he joked.

"You no make laugh," she protested. "You make laugh, bad thing happen."

"I'm sorry. I won't die because I want to come back to see you tonight. I love you. Don't worry."

"I number one love you."

Clint, wearing his green combat uniform, hugged her tightly. Then he filled his canteen with water Lien had boiled and checked his rifle, even though he had cleaned it the night before. Pushing his sloppy green bush hat down on his head, he kissed Lien goodbye.

Helicopters landed at the pad next to the team house one-by-one to pick up Vietnamese soldiers and flew slowly to the northeast. The last helicopter, the command "slick," picked up Clint, Chuong and four Popular Force sergeants. Chuong gave them last minute instructions as they flew over the green and deceptively tranquil countryside.

The spy ring providing Clint and Chuong with daily information on VC activity believed a high ranking enemy official would be visiting the area. Four overloaded helicopters, with 46 grim faced South Vietnamese soldiers in all, headed toward their destination.

The "landing site" was a flooded rice patty. The helicopters hovered over the water. With the 'copters at their most vulnerable point, American pilots and gunners yelled, "Get out! Get out!" Clint admired the well armed South Vietnamese soldiers who reluctantly jumped into the muddy water, not knowing its depth. They leapt the two feet to the water's surface holding their breath. He imagined they were instantly relieved to discover that the turbid water only came to their knees.

Upon hitting the silty water the platoon leaders yelled at their men to form a wide line across the front and to march forward to the tree line 300 meters away. Clint recognized the formation as the most primitive form of combat, thousands of years old.

Once the infantrymen were spread out, a little Vietnamese banter ensued. The platoon leaders yelled at their men to shut up. The mud sucked at their ankles; grasses and vines resisting their forward progress.

To encourage them to move faster Clint joined the front line and gave arm signals to move forward.

Chuong caught up with him and grabbed his sleeve. "You let them die first. Officers should stay back. Maybe this water is mined."

Clint did as suggested. The water got deeper as they moved forward. The suction of the mud grew stronger. It was slow moving.

Two-thirds of the way to the tree line, one soldiers yelled out.

"What did he say?" Clint asked Chuong, who was walking beside him.

"He said we are being fired upon."

Before Clint could say another word rifle fire resounded all along the line of forward trudging soldiers. The officers in the rear of the formation ducked down to neck deep in the warm water to make themselves smaller targets while holding their rifles overhead to keep them from getting wet.

Everyone continued to move forward, the water getting deeper. The water became chest high on Clint while the shorter Vietnamese were bobbing on tiptoes in order to keep from drowning. The water soaked uniforms became very heavy. Flying ants stung the faces and upraise arms of the soldiers.

No one was hit by enemy fire. As they got closer to the tree line M-79 grenade launchers were employed and were answered by rifle fire from the tree line. Still no casualties.

"Thank God they're lousy shots," Clint yelled at Chuong over the din of gunfire.

"Maybe they trained in China," Chuong responded with a scoffing look on his face.

By now the shortest Vietnamese had to be held up by their armpits to keep them from drowning.

Fighting both the enemy and the swamp Clint decided to use superior firepower to dislodge the unseen enemy. He called in helicopter gun ships, which quickly appeared over the horizon behind them and flew disconcertingly low overhead, aiming their big cannons at the tree line. Clint's heart missed a beat as the guns opened fire at the rate of 1,300 rounds per minute. With their zip zip zipping guns they mowed down the trees and hopefully anyone hiding in them. Still the line of men moved forward.

As they advanced it was realized that the line of trees was the bank of a small irrigation canal. Some of the soldiers who reached the line of trees first, shouted that there were footprints in the mud marking the quick escape of the VC.

Once on shore two abandoned shacks were searched. No clues were left behind. Two soldiers, who somehow still had lit cigarettes, set the hooches ablaze.

Then someone shouted that three men were running from the area. Shots were fired in their direction but the escapees soon disappeared into the underbrush.

Clint called for the two gun ships again. Smoke grenades were deployed to mark the location of friendly troops so the pilots would not mistake them for the VC. The gun ships dove and swooped to the location of the fleeing VC and mowed down more vegetation with their instruments of death.

With the danger from the enemy passed, a pile of freshly hewed pungy stakes were found on shore and a little sampan was discovered in the canal. Soldiers blasted the little boat and it quickly sank. The wooden spikes were kicked and scattered.

The intelligence squad searched slowly, groping through brush, vines, and mud but they found no more clues of the enemy.

It was another meaningless walk in the sun and the wading in water for the soldiers, Clint thought. They had been through this drill many times before. Soon the PF soldiers were picking oranges off trees, pulling down unripe bananas from vines, asking around for dry cigarettes, and making jokes. Clint expressed concern that this would be the ideal time for a counter-attack by the enemy but Chuong said it was unlikely.

Then the intelligence squad found a mine on the canal bank. About half the soldiers had walked over the trip wire without the mine exploding. This was treated as a hilarious incident by the Vietnamese soldiers.

The gun ships had gone back to refuel and now their return to the battle scene could be heard. Clint called off the operation.

The soldiers retreated back through the swamp, through the mud and stingy ants, and to high ground where a flare was set so the four helicopters could transport them back to Lap Vo.

Clint estimated the outing cost about $70,000. The results were one sunken sampan, one mine disabled, one pile of pungy stakes scattered, two shacks burned, oranges and bananas eaten, and three frightened VC.

Late that afternoon Lien greeted Clint with a big smile on her delicate face and tears in her big brown eyes.

CHAPTER 21
"Losing the war"

<u>Lap Vo, South Vietnam, 1970</u>

A special day was approaching and the team scrounged and saved for a month to collect the right items. Acquiring the proper ingredients took two excursions to the commissary in Sa Dec. Thanksgiving dinner in the middle of a rural Vietnam wetland was not easy to put together.

All the big military units in the country were going to have a traditional Thanksgiving dinner prepared by trained chefs, with walls decorated with pictures of turkeys and pilgrims, tables covered with white linen; but the three-man Lap Vo Team had to fend for itself.

The first thought was to save gasoline for the generator in order to have electricity for lighting and the refrigerator.

After careful planning Captain Roy presented the menu:

Thanksgiving in Vietnam
Menu

Beer and Pretzels
Vietnamese Salad Supreme
Dressing a la Angelo
Roy's Baked Turkey
Cranberry Sauce

Baked Potato
Clint's Ginger Bread withWhipped Cream
More Beer

If it were rationed, there was enough food to invite some Vietnamese friends. Everyone was allotted three handfuls of pretzels, one turkey breast, salad picked from wild growing plants identified as edible by Vietnamese women, a third of a can of cranberry sauce, one baked potato wrapped in tinfoil, a big helping of ginger bread with one table spoonful of whipped cream, and an unlimited supply of beer and Fresca.

Lien helped prepare the meal but she required close supervision to prevent her from adding *nuoc mam* to everything.

The Vietnamese friends and their children unexpectedly arrived on time for dinner. They liked the ginger bread and the salad and ate a polite amount of turkey and potato but could not stand the cranberry sauce. Everyone liked the beer and stayed until evening to help the team reduce their supply.

It was enjoyable to watch the Vietnamese children play games of tag while relaxing with their parents. Evidently their moms and dads told them to be well-mannered and not pull the hairs off American arms. Other than that, the children, wearing white shirts and black slacks or skirts, had the run of the place. Clint noticed the kids getting their hands and knees dirty on the cement floor but their parents did not seem to mind.

Major Alonzo tried to explain the meaning of Thanksgiving to the guests with the help of an interpreter. They were somewhat confused about eating with Indians until Alonzo reminded them of the American cowboy and Indian movies they had seen.

One of the Vietnamese men asked, "Are we now the Indians?"

The questioned was followed by a pause. Any answer could have been easily misunderstood, so Alonzo walked over and gave the man a big bear hug. Everyone laughed and applauded.

The generator decided to quit working at about 10 o'clock. Flashlights and candles were quickly deployed but the Vietnamese took this as a sign that it was time leave. With bows and handshakes they thanked the Americans for a wonderful time.

Lien quickly began washing the dishes and making sure everyone had a beer in their hand. When she began to sweep the floor Clint stopped her. Then she sat down beside him and had a beer too. After a couple sips she reached over and took his hand.

After she finished her beer Lien and Clint walked home together in the rain. When they passed through the compound gate a couple guards said something in Vietnamese and laughed.

"What did they say?" Clint asked.

"They be number 10. It be OK."

It softly rained all night and the temperature plummeted to the low 70's. Vietnamese call it the perfect weather for lovemaking. And it was.

The road to Sa Dec was washed out for the second time in two days. That meant no mail from home but also reduced the chances for inspections from higher command stationed in Sa Dec or Can Tho.

When Clint arrived at the team house the next morning the major seemed to be in a jovial mood. "Remember that crooked village chief who sold the materials to build bridges in his village?" he asked.

"How could I forget," Clint said. "You made a public spectacle of that asshole."

"He paid the money back to us yesterday!"

"I don't believe it."

"But I suspect the money really came from the district chief, who was on the take too. The money was used to buy more cement and gravel to finish the bridges."

"So things worked out after all?" Clint asked.

"Well, not quite," Angelo said. "The new village chief for Hoi An Dong presented us with a bill for the sand and cement he said he had to purchase."

Clint, with a quizzical look, said, "I thought you said the needed sand and cement was purchased after the stolen supplies were paid for."

"It was but I guess the district chief got control of the building materials again and sold them to the village. Now the village chief wants to be reimbursed. Not only that, the bill showed greatly inflated prices. The new village chief is either padding the bill for his own benefit or for the district chief or both," Angelo explained.

"So, what're we doing about it?"

"Well, Clint, we're not paying for our own supplies. We told the new village chief that he didn't go through the proper American advisors to be reimbursed," Angelo said. "For one thing, we're not sure the materials arrived at the sites and in their proper amounts. And another thing, we suspect that the district chief is just trying to get compensated for the money he had to pay out for the old village chief."

"This is getting confusing," Clint said.

"That's not all. The new village chief has also signed a contract with a rock company to buy 62,000 *dong* of rock. I'd guess that's about half a year's salary for him."

"Where's he getting the money?" asked Clint.

"I have no idea!" Angelo exclaimed. "First, I want to make sure the materials we already sent got where they are supposed to go. Wouldn't that be a pisser if we had to pay for our own supplies twice?"

"I'm getting more confused every minute," Clint said.

"Confusion is a smokescreen for graft. I think the new village chief is acting on behalf of the district chief. The district chief is trying to get back the money he had to return for the supplies skimmed on the original projects."

Clint said, "I'm not sure I follow you. But what're we going to do?"

"You know how inefficient bureaucracy can be. If any additional payments are expected, we can keep delaying at least until another district chief is appointed," Angelo said. "Which may be sooner than he thinks."

"All this corruption makes me sick," Clint said.

"Here's another little tidbit. I learned that several PF soldiers are getting platoon leaders pay even though they don't command platoons and have very soft jobs. For example, three soldiers are assigned to keeping their generator running. And one of them is considered a 'platoon leader.' The work is only about an hour per day for two soldiers and one supervisor. Since they have so much free time they have businesses in the market too. The catch is, they have to kickback much of their military pay to the district chief."

"You're still making me sick," Clint said.

"Here's another one," Angelo said. "The intel squad has 12 men; one is a fulltime supply sergeant, ridiculous. I bet there's another payoff there. There's a lot more going on like this than we'll ever uncover. The American brass doesn't give a shit anyway."

"I'm glad my job is to count bodies and not money," Clint said.

"There're only so many platoon leader slots. Since these are filled by graft the real platoon leaders get assistant platoon leader pay. So, the assistant platoon leaders are left with a privates' pay."

Clint asked, "So the district chief gets part of every platoon leaders pay?"

"You got it. Here's another one," Angelo said.

"I don't think I can take any more of this," Clint said.

"I guess I'm ruining your day but I thought I better let you know about this one," Angelo said.

"I can't wait."

"Being a gate guard is a very soft job."

"And that position is for sale too."

"You catch on pretty quick for a brand new captain. The position has a going price. One of our interpreters bought his brother-in-law a gate guard job. And they only work four hours per day!"

"I'm so glad we're so well protected."

"There is even a program for draft dodgers. They're hired as spies or 'agents.'"

"Hey, you're talking about my boys now."

"They sit around in cafes all day and pick up a rumor or

make one up every couple days. That's all they need to do to keep their jobs. These men and women are hired directly by the district chief. And of course there is a kickback to the chief," Angelo said.

"I hope the district chief has a bookkeeper to keep track of all this graft. It sounds to me like the only people who have dangerous jobs are those who're so poor they can't pay anyone for a safer position," Clint concluded.

"You're so right. You've seen them. They're the soldiers shooting the river rats and taking them home to feed the family. If you walk outside our compound right now you'll find some poor slobs in soldiers' fatigues combing the canals looking for dinner," Angelo said with disgust.

"Lien told me not to eat the rats because it makes your muscles ache."

"I'll keep that in mind."

"All this means low morale for the South Vietnamese military. People don't want to fight for a system that treats them unfairly."

"Yep."

"That's why we're losing the war," Clint said.

"Anyone who says they understand what's going on in Vietnam is either delusional or a fool."

"I assure you, Major Alonzo, I don't fall into either of those categories."

CHAPTER 22

Covert operations

For Clint the Vietnam War was a hodgepodge of secret documents, covert operations and underhanded deals. Every Phoenix Advisor experienced a crash course in "black ops" and dirty tricks. But appearance was always more important than substance.

He was also dealing with some personal issues. The day was approaching when he knew he would have to say 'goodbye' to Lien. He tried to bring up this delicate subject to her a couple times but she refused to discuss it. The language barrier between the two did not make the discussion any easier. Her typical response was, "You no leave. I go with you."

"I love you but I can't take you with me," he would respond.

Then she would shout, "You Number 10! You no love me!" She would pout for hours and resist Clint's attempts to comfort her.

The situation upset and saddened him. He felt helpless but also realized he had to keep his mind on his job. Distraction or inattention could get him killed. He had to remain alert for snipers and mines. Many in his position had met their demise simply by neglecting to observe someone hiding in a tree or the telltale sign of disturbed ground where a mine may have been set.

One day, on short notice, Clint was called to an Army Intelligence office in Can Tho. He met with someone dressed as a major and with the shiny crossed pistols emblem on his collar. The officer did not introduce himself but his name tag said "Smith." The crisp looking man withdrew a pair of handcuffs and locked one end of the cuffs around Clint's left wrist. The other end was attached to the handle of a locked briefcase.

"That's not too tight is it?"

"No sir; it's fine."

"Someone will meet you at the airport in Saigon who has the key. When he gives you the password, you surrender the briefcase to him. He'll unlock the handcuffs and keep both the cuffs and the briefcase."

"The password?"

The major took a slip of onion skin paper from his desk, wrote the password and response on it and turned it so Clint could read the words.

Clint nodded.

The major then put the scrap of paper in the ash tray and lit it. It flamed briefly and disappeared.

"I don't have to tell you not to allow anyone else to attempt to open this case. If you do, you, he and the Top Secret documents inside will be blown into tiny pieces. There won't be much left of you to put in a body bag," he said with a chuckle.

"Yes, sir," Clint said and smiled.

It was the first of several courier trips Clint would make for the CIA.

On the way back to Can Tho from his first classified document delivery, riding a helicopter skimming over tree tops, Clint unexpectedly spotted a hut flying the Viet Cong flag.

"Look at that flag up ahead! Let's get us a war trophy," Clint yelled to the pilot.

"You're crazy? I'm not landing next to a hooch with an enemy flag," the pilot responded.

"Who said anything about landing? We can snag it from the air."

Already past the target, the pilot, wanting to demonstrate his flying skill Clint surmised, swooped back toward the red and blue flag with a big yellow star in the middle. "You lean out and grab it when we get close."

Clint, in turn, looked at the gunner and said, "I'll hold you by the belt and you lean out and grab the flag."

"Yes, sir," the enlisted man said with a big grin on his face.

The helicopter hovered closer and closer to the shack with the VC flag fluttering over its roof. Despite the shaking and air turbulence, Clint was able to hold the enlisted man by his belt as he extended his upper body and arms into mid-air. Just as the gunner was about to clutch the flag the violent downdraft created by the chopper shook the small building. The lightly constructed shanty ripped apart in seconds. The flag disappeared into a pile of rubble.

Amidst ineffective gunfire the chopper sped away. No trophy that day. Laughing, the pilot said he would report 'one VC dwelling destroyed.'

The word "pacification" was a favorite term used by the military bureaucracy. The meaning was quite flexible and took many forms. It could mean crushing guerrilla resistance with bullets and bombs. It could also mean crafting a stable social and economic system that would demonstrate to the populace the benefits offered by the Saigon government.

Sitting in the Officers' Club in Can Tho, nursing a beer and enjoying the air conditioning, Clint learned about a "pacification" operation that was unique in its scope to garner favorable publicity while being meaningless to the total war effort.

A young officer he had trained with plopped down beside him and said, "Hi Clint. What you up to?"

"Sitting here wishing we had air conditioning in Lap Vo."

"Where's that?"

"Up the river from here. It's a little village in Sa Dec Province."

"I bet you're doing more for the war effort than I am."

"I'm not sure about that. My major accomplishment this week was to totally destroy some poor farmer's house."

"See, I knew you were doing more to advance the cause of freedom than me."

"What do you mean?"

"You know the highway from Can Tho to An Xuyen Province? It's a death trap and every soldier on the ground knows it. The only way to get from this province capital to the next is by air."

"Yeah, so?"

"The famous newspaper columnist, Stewart Alsop, evidently heard differently. He told some general he wanted to personally drive that road so he could write an article on the accomplishments of the pacification program for his readers.

He got his drive and his story."

"How could that be?"

"With my help. His column, based on his personal experience, glowingly expressed increasing security in the Delta Region."

"And what's the real story?"

"He drove that highway all right. Just like he wanted. What he was unaware of was the mine sweepers and armor unit that preceded him and the tanks that followed him down that road, just out of his sight. There were also troops in blocking positions all along the roadway to prevent any ambushes of his Jeep."

"Yeah?"

"Because of me, and a thousand other men of course, he was completely safe that day. For one day the highway was safe. The next day it became one of the most dangerous highways in Vietnam again."

"Would you like to escort me back to Lap Vo?"

"No, but I'll buy you the next beer."

Clint and Lien spent Christmas in Can Tho where they could find a Christmas dinner and cold beer. Since Clint was spending so much time in Can Tho, Lien preceded him on this trip to rent an apartment for them.

Lien found the housing costs much higher in Can Tho. But she figured a way to cut costs. She rented the one-room apartment from the legal renter, not from the landlord. She told the landlord that she was the daughter of the renter and she would be moving in with her mother. The South

Vietnamese law stipulated that rental costs could not increase until there was a change of renters. Lien made an agreement with the renter to keep the renter's name the lease for a small monthly fee, thus allowing the rent to stay the same. Inflation was wreaking havoc on the economy, but not for Lien and Clint when it came to renting an apartment in Can Tho.

When Lien explained to Clint what she had done, he exclaimed, "You broke the rent control laws!"

"I don't know what you say. I no break law."

"OK. I guess you're just smart."

"Yes, I smart," she said.

The next day Clint heard, that while they were enjoying their holiday, about 350 soldiers, who were promised Christmas at home in the U.S., were sorely disappointed.

Although the soldiers got to Saigon, they spent Christmas Eve in the drab Tan Son Nhut Airport instead. Their Boeing 747, to take them back to America, was not allowed to land even though the airfield was equipped for landing big jets.

The U.S. Embassy said the problem was of a "technical and jurisdictional nature." Clint told Lien that that was diplomatic speech. "It really meant that the plane could not land because the right people were not bribed, or not bribed in the expected amount."

"I don't know what you say. Everybody pay taxes. Gov'ment people charge tax so babysauns can eat. You say that no good?"

"It's more complicated than that."

"Not what you say. You no Vietnamee."

Clint took Lien in his arms. "You're right. I don't always understand the culture. I love you."

"I love you too. I sorry say you no love."

By now bribery was becoming a way-of-life for Clint too. Not all Vietnamese wanted to play this game, however. Clint learned of a well-liked South Vietnamese sergeant who was well qualified to become an officer but did not get his deserved promotion because he would not pay a kickback. Clint took up a secret collection among American officers to pay for the sergeant's promotion and his advancement was quickly approved. The new officer was never told of the helping hand provided him, so was happy to believe he rose in rank due to his own abilities.

That was one small secret compared to some very big secrets. When Clint escorted some captives to a Vietnamese prison in Can Tho he learned that major and minor criminals were housed together and there was no segregation of prisoners based on age or sex. Sometimes entire families were jailed together even though only one member of the family broke the law. When Clint complained of such treatment his concern was relayed to John Vann. When Vann took a look for himself he said his greatest concern was that the New York Times would learn about these conditions and publish an article about it.

Sometimes even small secrets can affect a lot of people. The American commander of the Vinh Long Airfield decided to establish an eight o'clock curfew for the adjacent city. All soldiers and airmen had to be on base by the designated time. This restriction was met with great disfavor.

Clint and another young army officer were discussing the new curfew in the Vinh Long Officers' Club one night when they observed the base commander finish his drink and leave the club. They watched him exit the compound and walk across the street to where his girlfriend lived. Clint had the same kind of arrangement in Lap Vo.

They waited until nine o'clock and then told the military police that they believed a G.I. was illegally off-post in a house just across the street from the front gate.

The military police commander, anxious to prove himself, organized a raid on the house. Talk about getting caught with your pants down!

The next day the curfew was lifted.

American company grade officers were becoming increasing concerned about 'fragging,' retaliation by enlisted men directed toward their officers. Fragging was just another word for attempted or actual murder of officers for maintaining discipline or for giving orders that may put their men in danger. The favored means of fragging was by rolling a hand grenade into the officer's living quarters, usually when they were asleep. Perpetrators were rarely caught and punished.

South Vietnamese officers were much more concerned about this practice than their American counterparts. These acts were typically blamed on Viet Cong sabotage, since no one had time to investigate murder in a combat zone where death often came quickly and unexpectedly. It was much easier to blame the deaths on the enemy.

One province chief was ambushed by "VC" in Phong Dinh Province along a frequently traveled road in broad daylight and within sight of a Regional Forces outpost. Complaints and power struggles were often settled in this manner.

The practice of fragging was so commonplace that South Vietnamese officers begged and clambered to be transported by American helicopters with American pilots, not by their own troops. Americans were willing to accommodate the South Vietnamese officers whenever convenient or part of a joint operation.

The number of murders perpetrated by soldiers and civilians will never be known. The CIA readily recognized that incompetence, corruption, and questionable loyalty could easily be handled with violence, and the VC would be the easy scapegoat.

On one of his trips to Can Tho, Clint was called into the office of a superior officer. He had a large battery-looking device on his desk.

"General Tri is flying to Tay Ninh City at 1400 hours this afternoon," he told Clint. "I want you to deliver this battery to his helicopter just before it takes off. You won't have any trouble getting through security to deliver it."

"This doesn't sound like something an officer would normally do," Clint questioned.

"The general is not going to trust a Vietnamese soldier to deliver it but he would trust an American officer. Tell him the battery is needed for the troops he is visiting in Tay Ninh and ask him if it would be all right to put it on board."

"Why would a battery be transported in this manner?"

"You don't have a need to know."

"Anything else, sir?"

"Handle this battery carefully. It's sensitive equipment. Also, you don't remember how this battery got on board."

"Sir?"

"I'm trying to maintain plausible deniability for you."

"Yes sir. I understand."

The boundary of Cambodia juts into Vietnam just west of Saigon. This area, which resembled a parrot's beak on the map, militarily had to be treated as part of Vietnam to in order to protect the city from invasion. The flamboyant and highly decorated Lieutenant General Do Cao Tri, called the "Patton of the Parrot Beak," became the latest high ranking South Vietnam officer to be a casualty of war. His helicopter blew up and crashed before reaching its destination. Nine South Vietnamese soldiers perished with him. News reports said the 'copter in which he was traveling had a serious mechanical malfunction.

CHAPTER 23

News from 'Nam

The private life between Clint and Lien was in turmoil. They spent less time making love and more time embracing each other and crying. They did not want to leave each other but the inevitable was approaching.

When Lien was not crying, she was pouting. Clint felt helpless, frustrated, and guilty. When they met and fell in love it seemed like it would last forever. Now a life without each other seemed forever. It was not a happy time.

The world seemed to be in turmoil too. In the *Stars and Stripes* newspaper Clint read that someone named Charles Manson and three others were convicted of the brutal murder of actress Sharon Tate, her husband, and five of their friends. He also read that seven thousand anti-war demonstrators were arrested in Washington D.C. The Weather Underground claimed responsibility for a bomb blast that ripped into a U.S. Senate restroom causing $300,000 in damage. And First Lieutenant William Calley was found guilty of murdering 22 Vietnamese civilians.

Clint never discussed the My Lai Massacre with Lien. He could not understand it himself. Explaining to her how this could happen was impossible. He was grateful that she never mentioned it. Maybe she did not know. Maybe she had heard of it but thought it was one of the outcomes of war. She had seen and heard about many horrible inhumanities in her short life.

Yet, she was a gentle and loving person. Clint did not know how this could be possible but found himself fortunate to have found her. Now he was leaving her and felt returning to the U.S. diminished them both.

Who are we to believe we can teach the Vietnamese a higher form of civilization? Clint thought. *We want to be the kingmakers but we have not stopped to learn and understand their culture. We don't understand our friends or our enemies in Vietnam and this will be our downfall.*

In Washington D.C. plans were being made to turn all military ground operations over to the South Vietnamese Army. It was believed that the "Vietnamization" phase of the war was doing quite well. South Vietnamese operations against the battle hardened North Vietnamese were considered to be generally successful, it was said. *Unrealistically optimistic intelligence reports have finally come to their illogical conclusion,* Clint thought.

In little Lap Vo, Clint said to Lien, "I'm concerned about what will happen to you if the communist takeover."

"You leave me. Why you care?"

"Please listen to me. If the communist take over how many supporters of the United States would be punished?"

"America no leave."

"Yes, we're leaving. There are fewer Americans here all the time."

"Maybe me go America," she said.

"All the South Vietnamese can't go to America. Only those

with influence would be able to leave Vietnam. What about the rest of the people?"

"Me don't know what you say. You no leave me or you take me."

"I will write you letters," he said.

"Me write you too," she said with tears in her eyes, beginning to accept reality. "Me know someone who read letters you for me and help me write you. She write American nice."

"If writing to you puts you in danger, then I won't be able to write you."

"Can send you picture too," she said. "Send you picture boy of me."

"If the communists take over I will not be able to write."

"Vietnamee no tell how they feel. Not me. Me say love you. Me tell boy of me you his father. Me show him picture you."

Now tears came to his eyes too.

They held each other, their hearts crumbling.

Although they knew the day of his departure from Vietnam for weeks, when the day would come, Clint knew it would be a dreadful day they would never forget.

Clint remembered the time Lien told him she would rather be American than Vietnamese. *She will try to escape the communists. She might die trying.*

Tillamook, Oregon, USA, 1972

A year later the news Clint was getting from Vietnam was

not good. It was reported that the supplies flowing southward on the Ho Chi Minh Trail were increasing.

The American bombing in Cambodia was not stopping the food, medicine, guns and ammunition carried in tunnels, on bicycles, and on the backs of human beings. The ARVN were losing their grip on the highlands and the northern provinces.

An Army buddy called Clint.

"Hello . . ."

"Hey, man. You been keepin' up on the news from 'Nam?"

"Yeah, what about it."

"It looks like the South is gettin' their ass kicked, just like you predicted."

"Shit, what now?"

"Ol' President Thieu ordered General Phu, the II Corps commander, out of the highlands."

"I was never there," Clint responded.

"But it's still part of South Vietnam, right?"

"Yeah."

"Well listen to this: the general delegated the job to his assistants. Then he and his staff flew directly to lovely Nha Trang leavin' his poor grunts to fend for themselves. The fucked up retreat became a 135 mile shootin' gallery for the North Vietnam Army. Not only was the highway to the coast mined, it was covered with mortar and machine gun fire and . . ."

"Shit, I'm glad Lien's not there."

"Shut up and listen, man. When the South Vietnamese Army retreated, thousands of family members and civilians followed. The military convoy was slowed down by buses, trucks, cars, motor scooters, bicycles, oxcarts, and peasants carryin' everythin' they owned on their backs."

"How do you know all this?"

"You got to read more than the front page of the newspaper and watchin' the news on TV. At a place called Cheo Reo the people in the column fell easy prey to mutinous Montagnards."

"I knew when the South Vietnamese pilots dropped their extra bombs on the Montagnards, their own people, it was going to piss 'em off," Clint said.

"The slaughter of ARVN and civilians . . . well they shot everyone. Children and the old folks weren't spared. This could happen to Lien someday. Maybe soon."

"Thanks for that nice thought."

"Let me read somethin' to ya. A news reporter calls it 'the Convoy of Tears.' I'm quotin' here now: 'The sound of roaring artillery and small arms, the scream of the seriously wounded people at death's door, and children, created a voice out of hell.'"

"What does the North have to gain by killing everyone?"

"Fuck if I know. Here's some more: their escape was halted for five days when the NVA blew up the bridge over the Song Ba River. Soldiers and civilians were mowed down by machine guns when they tried to surrender. Others drowned tryin' to swim across the river. While bodies floated down the river survivors were reduced to eatin' roots and grass to stay alive. . . ."

"You sure know how to brighten my day."

Well, I gotta git goin.' Some of us have ta work for a livin'. You still lookin' for a job?"

"Yeah."

"Maybe you should've taken that job with the CIA."

"Yeah, maybe I should've. Maybe they would have sent me back to Vietnam so I could protect Lien."

"Yeah, and got your ass shot off by a bunch of gooks."

"You know I don't like that word."

"Sorry, man. See ya later."

"Yeah, thanks again . . ."

"Any time buddy. Later."

Mountain Rest, South Carolina, USA, 2004

Clint reached down to pet his golden retriever. All this thought of Vietnam was making him depressed. And thirsty.

"If I could only train you to go fetch the beer . . . and open the bottle. Then I'd have a valuable dog," Clint said as he sat in his blue Adirondack chair on his back deck.

The big brown eyed dog looked up at him with an expression; *I'll do anything for you. But first I have to understand what you want.*

"The war was a long time ago. A lifetime ago."

CHAPTER 24

Most Important Decision

<u>South Vietnam, 1975</u>

It did not take long for American supporters in Vietnam to experience the cruelty of their new rulers. Many were thrown into 'tiger cages' or prohibited from owning businesses. The freedom the South Vietnamese enjoyed with the American occupation swiftly came to an end.

The South Vietnamese engaged in passive resistance but the oppression was pervasive. Ironically, much of the South Vietnamese leadership had actually come from the North. Now the new leadership came from the North also, but with a much different philosophy.

Clint had suspected that Lien would become one of the "Boat People." *Where would she go? How would she survive? How come I never heard from her again?*

<u>An Giang, Vietnam, 1976</u>

"You must go too," Lien told her father, a long retired military officer who had fought with the French.

"No, my child. I am too old," he said.

"The communist will put you in jail. Maybe they will work you to death."

"I would rather die in Vietnam, not in the ocean to be eaten by the fish."

"I may never see you again," Lien said as she wept.

"You need to take care of your boy and give him a future. You should not have to take care of an old man too. Take care of your son so he can become a successful American," he encouraged her.

Lien put her hands together and bowed low to her father. He took her in his arms, something he rarely did, and she leaned against his bony chest. His gray stringy beard touched the top of her head.

Lien's beloved An Giang Province was in a state of confusion. It was a province so loyal to the government of South Vietnam there had not been any American soldiers stationed there. In the face of communism many thought about leaving the province. But, situated in the middle of the Mekong Delta, a coastal escape seemed a long way away for most people.

Lien, however, was tired of living in fear. Fear was her constant companion since the communist assumed control. She was not political but she was known to be a friend to an American. All it would take is for a jealous neighbor to point her out as a trouble-maker to the police in order to send her to 'reeducation camp,' where she would be forced into slave labor.

Her province, village and hamlet officials were captured and summarily executed. She knew farmers who lost their land to resettlement. Businessmen lost their livelihoods because they had traded with Americans. Disgruntled peasants were drafted into the Army to fight Cambodia. Her elderly father was under constant surveillance.

New settlers on the land, loyal to the communists, did not

know how to farm. Educated professionals were not allowed to return to their occupations. The communists appropriated needed supplies from businesses.

Collective farms and workshops failed. People went hungry, an uncommon experience in South Vietnam.

Former supporters of the South Vietnam government were not welcome in the new government or the economy. Surveillance of the population in the South was relentless.

The country fell into economic depression.

For Lien, it was time to leave. If she did not, life would become even more difficult for her and her half-American son.

She thought the best place from which to escape the country was Vung Tau, where she had met Clint and had some friends. Lien's parents paid a shadowy figure in gold for her secret passage out of the country. Lien also sold all of her jewelry but did not get very much money for it. Cash was needed to bride the soldiers at check points, to pay for bus fare and to buy food in Vung Tau.

A half dozen young people left An Giang together very early one morning. They found separate seats on the old bus, not wanting to look like they were escaping together. They sat and waited for the bus to fill up. An hour later the bus was packed with peasants, crying babies, flapping chickens with their feet tied together, late comers hanging off the back, and rowdy boys on top of the roof.

Down the highway they jolted. The heat and the smells inside the bus rose by the minute. All the windows were open in the bus but this provided little relief, only a coating of dust mixed with diesel fumes.

On the way to Vung Tau, they passed through five road

blocks where the passengers were inspected for identification and weapons. Each time they were stopped, a small bribe was extracted from each adult passenger. Twice on the trip the bus halted in a rural area for a bathroom break where women squatted in the tall grass on the left side of the bus and the men rolled up their baggy pant leg and relieved themselves on the right side of the bus. Then the bus driver honked his horn and people scrambled to retrieve their seats.

In Lien's woven blue and white plastic satchel she carried a large vegetable can filled with cooked rice, a glass jar of drinking water, and one change of underwear for herself and her little son. She knew she would be allowed only one small carry-on for the ocean trip.

From the bus window everything appeared normal, unchanged. But she knew the people she saw were hungry and frightened, just like her. The countryside opened into emerald green rice paddies, fish ponds bordered by palm trees and coconut. White cranes flitted over the fields which were often inhabited by dark colored menacing looking water buffaloes. Children walked along the highways, wearing white shirts with a red kerchief tied at the neck. Some of the boys stopped along the way to play a quick game of soccer in their bare feet.

Getting close to Vung Tau, the city she loved, looked shockingly different. She remembered it as a hectic place with slow traffic, honking horns, swirling eddies of Hondas, Vespas, oxcarts, and rickshaws. Pollution belching trucks and two-stroke engine scooters no longer caused women and some men to cover their faces with scarves. She remembered someone saying once, "We have become a country to Muslims now." Lien remembered that joke with a smile.

Now it was a city with pock-marked walls, machine guns set up at street corners, and bicycles instead of scooters. Once a vibrant city of shipping, tourism, and fine restaurants, it was now grim and quiet. People looked down as they walked, avoiding eye contact.

Late afternoon the bus passengers arrived in Vung Tau weary and dirty. Lien splurged on a cheap hotel room where she and her son could bathe and wash their clothes for the trip the next night. In the market they bought fried rice with bits of pork and cabbage wrapped in a banana leaf.

She violated curfew to meet a man in a dark corner near the market who gave her strict instructions to meet at a specific dock at an exact time. Then he handed her a coded receipt.

Leaving Vietnam was the most important decision of her life. She knew the trip was fraught with danger. The captain could easily steal her money. The boat could be captured by the Vietnamese Navy. The vessel could be unseaworthy and sink at the first hint of a storm, or run out of fuel and be washed ashore. The marauding Thai pirates could steal what little they had, rape the women, and murder all those who might be witnesses to their cruelty. Lien had heard that some escape boats simply floated out into the ocean until the passengers died of dehydration and starvation.

Even if they made it to some foreign shore, they could be sent back to Vietnam where they would be imprisoned as traitors.

There best hope was to be rescued by an American or Australian ship.

CHAPTER 25

One of the Boat People

In the small dimly lit hotel room Lien unfolded a document from her purse. On it were two black and white "mug shots," one of herself and the other of Clint. Attached was a gold foil seal and ribbon. It had also been pounded with a rubber stamp with red ink, and illegibly signed by three people. In bold, it said in Vietnamese that Tran Thi Lien and Clinton McGregor could legally cohabit in Can Tho Province, Republic of Vietnam.

She remembered the frightening night when the officious looking government certificate saved her from abuse and possible imprisonment. In their Can Tho apartment, she and Clint were awakened at two o'clock in the morning by pounding on their door and yelling in Vietnamese. Clint woke up with a start and grabbed his rifle.

"You no shoot," Lien yelled. "I open door."

"No," he said. "What's going on?"

"You no yell. Soldiers look for VC. We no answer door, they break door and shoot us."

"Those sons-of-bitches. I'm an Army officer."

"You be quiet. You want I should die?"

Lien opened the door and five armed South Vietnamese soldiers barged in. They looked at Lien with a leer and scowled at Clint. They pointed to pictures on the wall, turned over furniture, rummaged for something to eat or drink, and crowded Lien into a corner.

Clint was fuming. "Get out!" he demanded. "Who the hell do you think you are?"

They did not understand a thing he said, so they just laughed at him.

"I say you no talk. I talk," Lien shouted at Clint. "You talk more they take me away and call me VC. They do what they want to me. Maybe you no see me again."

Clint was so angry he was shaking. He did not say another word, but handed the one who seemed in charge his Army Intelligence identification pass with his picture on it that said he could travel anywhere in the country at any time and could not be detained.

The South Vietnamese sergeant grabbed the plastic coated wallet-sized card, scoffed, dropped to the floor and stepped on it. Clint took a half step toward him, looked down at his tormentor, and the soldier took a step back.

Finally, Lien was able to dissuade the soldiers from their irrational aggression, went to the little table next to the bed, and pulled out the co-habitation permit. She pointed to Clint's photo and then to Clint. Then she said something in Vietnamese, bowed, and gave all the men a beautiful smile.

The sergeant gave an order and his men filed out of the apartment. The government document saved her from being declared a VC, she did not have to pay a bribe, and the soldiers stole nothing from the apartment. Lien was back to sleep within a half hour but Clint could not sleep the rest of the night.

She remembered how angry Clint had become. Lien knew

Clint had been frustrated because he had no way to protect the one he loved. The incident seemed like a long time in the past, but in reality it was just four years ago.

Lien realized it had been foolish to still keep the co-habitation permit. If any of the new government officials found it, it would be evidence enough to send her to a communist reeducation camp. But she could not part with it; her last real connection to Clint. She rolled the document as tightly as possible, flattened the roll, and then crammed it into the toe of her shoe.

Now, approaching midnight, Lien gathered her few belongings, told her young son to be quiet, and silently shut the hotel room door behind them. It was still warm and humid but there was a slight refreshing breeze blowing from the east. She held his little hand as they slowly walked down the alley to the docks in the dark. The boy's sandals slapped on the stone walkway.

"I told you to be quiet. Walk quietly or I will have to carry you," she whispered.

"I don't want to be carried. I want to walk."

"Then walk quietly and quit stumbling."

She loved her half-American son and felt guilty for taking out her anxiety on him. She would sacrifice everything for him; maybe she was, she thought.

Many Boat People, she knew, were returned by foreign governments to Vietnam. The returnees were dealt with harshly, including being worked to death on construction projects. There were many things needing repair in Vietnam and the communist rulers saw the "traitors" as a cheap source of labor. Lien wondered what would happen to her boy if she were caught; he would probably be put into an orphanage and neglected. There were many such orphanages in Vietnam now.

Her face was etched with fear and uncertainty. She was not the carefree and generally happy girl she had been. She was tired. Lien's slight frame ached from stress.

Lien held the hand of her son tighter and he flinched with pain. He did not complain. Lien believed he understood his mother would not hurt him on purpose. She knew her boy was old enough to know she was worried but not old enough to understand why they were quietly boarding a boat in the middle of the night. Getting on a fishing boat and going into the ocean would be fun, she told him. He had never seen the ocean but was told it was water so big he would not be able to see the shore on the other side.

Emerging from the shadows from every direction were other people walking silently toward the docks. They came in groups of two or three or four. The typical Vietnamese family might have eight or nine children but Lien understood that escaping Vietnam often meant separating families or leaving some family members behind. It might be too expensive to bring everyone. The tearing of the family apart was a cause of much debate and anguish within the families. Healthy young adults, like Lien, were the most likely to leave. The elderly and the sick were often left behind, usually by their own choice. They would help pay for the costly passage in order to make a better life for their children and grandchildren.

The cluster of escapees got bigger and more concentrated as they got closer to the docks. Still no one talked. This was the time they were most vulnerable to being detained by the authorities.

To the officials of the Socialist Republic of Vietnam it was embarrassing to have their people flee. They wanted international recognition and not be compared to East Germany, Cuba, or Haiti. Increasingly the national police ruthlessly stopped people from leaving the country. Timing, luck, and bribery of officials played important roles in escaping. And once escaped, not being sent back.

Lien's first goal was simply to leave the country. She had other goals too but they seemed distant and beyond her control. The destiny of her son and herself might be happiness and freedom. Or it could be starvation, drowning, disease, or to be murdered.

Her immediate hope was for rescue by the American Navy, sent to the United States and an opportunity to learn proper English. She wanted her son to go to a good school where he would not be taunted by the Vietnamese children for his blond hair. Her personal dream was to go to college. Such a silly thought almost made her smile.

And she wanted to find Clint. She could be his wife. If he could not marry her, she would be his mistress. The emotion of jealousy crept into her mind.

Maybe she would be sent to a refugee camp and stay there for years because no country wanted her. Maybe she would be captured by the Thai pirates; she did not want to think what they would do to her. She wondered if she would be given a choice of countries. *If I cannot go to the United States, Australia would be nice,* she thought. *There were a lot of Australians in Vung Tau and they always seemed friendly but often drunk.*

Near the dock now, someone bumped into her, jolting her back to reality. *Maybe I'm going crazy,* she thought. *First my son and I have to survive. There is no point in planning for the future now.*

This was not a time to let her mind wander, she reminded herself. Their future would be left to both fate and to her correct decisions. From now on she would be known as one of the "Boat People."

When Lien saw the old fishing boat she was about to board, almost unconsciously, she crossed herself. She was not Catholic but her father was. Her mother raised her as a Buddhist. The new regime did not like "the opiate of the masses," but they especially hated Catholics. The fisherman who owned this boat evidently was spiritual, like most other fisherman, because he had painted big eyes on the bow of the junk. Little else had been painted in recent years as evidenced by the gray weathered haul. The boat flew the SRV flag, a yellow star in a red field.

When Lien's little boy saw the flag he said, "*Tien quan ca* (Marching to the front)." He had learned the new national anthem in school. "Soldiers of Vietnam, we go forward . . .," he began to sing.

Lien shushed him.

The old boat, groaning against the hemp ropes that tied it to the dock, did not look seaworthy. Certainly this aged hulk would be abandoned once it reached its destination, wherever that may be. One possible resting place was at the bottom of the ocean far from land. Lien doubted that it would survive the mildest storm.

Lien questioned whether she had made the right decision. Certainly her son would be safer in her village than on this old fishing boat. She also realized it was still not too late to be cheated out of her money. Thieves had often taken gold from

Boat People but failed to provide the promised transportation. Also, police could be disguised as Boat People and could arrest them and throw them into prison, but not until they stole their money and possessions.

Her absence from her village had probably been discovered by now. Her parents, who gave everything they had to help finance the trip, would be roughly questioned by the authorities. Any of her property left behind, like her sleeping platform, cookware and nice dresses would be confiscated by the government.

At the dock the captain waved his arms to hurry the people onto his craft. It looked too small for the number of people arriving. She picked up her son, much to his objection, so he would not be trampled by people scurrying up the gangplank.

As she stepped onto the boat a man with a whistle around his neck glanced at her receipt and said, "Lady, you must pay 10,000 *dong* more to be on the deck."

"I cannot afford that," Lien protested.

"Then you go below. Down this ladder."

Lien breathed in some fresh air, then descended into the ship's hold. "Grab onto me around my neck," she told her son. At the bottom of the stairs she held him to her right hip with his legs on either side of her.

It was very dark and stifling. She could hear coughing and babies crying. Those behind her pushed her forward. She tripped over people in front of her and apologized.

The dock was lighted, allowing shafts of light between the separations in the planks above to pierce the darkness. Her eyes began to adjust. She saw the black silhouettes of people sitting on narrow benches. Holding her boy, she crowded into an empty space. It was uncomfortable but she assumed discomfort would only get worse.

As more and more people shuffled into the hold she realized she was fortunate to have a seat at all. Some squatted. Some lay on the floor. The ceiling was too low for most people to stand. An old man lay under Lien's bench groaning and farting.

Lien brought only rice and water as she was instructed. Her nose told her not everyone followed the rules. She smelled *pho* (noodle soup) and *cha gio* (egg role) but she was too nervous to be hungry anyway.

Vietnamese are normally unconcerned about crowded conditions, Clint had once told Lien. *They don't have the concept of "personal space" like Americans.* Nevertheless, Lien felt unsafe. Everyone was touching someone, breathing someone else's air, sweating on each other. They had not even left the dock yet and babies needed their diapers changed. If the boat began to sink or if there was a fire, they would all be trapped and unable to save themselves.

When the boat engine chugged to a start there was a murmur of relief, but soon diesel fumes permeated the already foul air and the engine noise made it difficult to converse or even think.

Lien wore loose fitting pajamas, the appropriate dress for these conditions, but she felt like a peasant. Her father had been an army officer, her family had owned land, her parents could speak French fluently, everyone in her family attended high school, but now she was sitting in steerage. She was not one of these people she told herself.

When conditions were dire, Lien had learned to mentally escape. There were times during the war when she found she could, in her mind, be someplace else. *Don't think of these uncomfortable, frightening conditions*, she told herself. *Think of something pleasant.* With an unseen twinkle in her eye she remembered how proud she was when she walked down Quang Trung Street in Vung Tau holding onto Clint's arm and wearing an expensive *ao dai*. The distinctive Vietnamese dress with a tight bodice and the long skirt split far up both sides showed off her natural beauty. Clint wore dark slacks and a white dress shirt that day. They went to a Korean restaurant on the waterfront. With a smile she remembered how surprised Clint was when she insisted on paying the bill. That day she felt like a liberated American woman.

There was a gush of enthusiasm in the boat when they hit the first ocean wave. They were truly on their way now; to where she was not quite sure.

Over the din of the engine some people cautiously began to talk and get acquainted. Lien kept quiet and listened. Many of the passengers, she learned, were from Vung Tau and Saigon. Most of the passengers were from along the coast and the Mekong Delta. More people began to ask, "Where are you from?" Lien heard people mention Vinh Long near her province, the big city of Can Tho, and also Long Thanh, My Tho, Tra Vinh, Bac Lieu and Ca Mau. The communist regime had brought all these people together who would have never met otherwise.

The people talked about how beautiful their part of Vietnam was before the war, how their leaders were treated when the communists took over, and how they were going to make a new life for themselves and their family. Lien noted some regional accents and the crude language of peasants.

Lien left with other young people from An Giang but she had not seen them on the boat.

The old man under Lien's bench did not say a word. His moaning became weaker and she wondered if he would be the first of many to die on this journey.

CHAPTER 26

"The Cap Blowing Off"

<u>South China Sea, 1976</u>

With a queasy stomach Lien realized she was satisfied not to
have eaten anything for hours. The old fishing boat endlessly
rolled side to side and front to back. In the dark it was hot and
humid and dusty and cramped. The smells and the sounds were
nearly overpowering. Stale food, rotting timbers, fresh puke,
and rank body odors permeated the air. Babies cried, older
people complained, the elderly groaned. The engine chugged
and the ancient planks of the vessel creaked, adding to the
ominous cacophony. The lack of oxygen made people drowsy.
The place had the feel of being buried alive while death came
slowly.

Surely, this will kill some people, Lien thought. *But I must not
die. I must live so my boy can live. Conserve my strength. Sleep if I can.
Don't let go of him. Protect him. Ration our water. Don't breathe too
deeply; it will make me gag.*

Minutes seemed like hours. Hours seemed like days. The
constant rocking, the verge of nausea, the incessant engine
noise, the smells both human and mechanical, made staying
calm a torture. *Remember to breathe, but not too much of this foul
air.*

Sleep provided some escape, but waking was a gradual
introduction to delayed torment. More nausea, sweating,

body odor, disorientation. *Where am I? Hell? I'm in hell. My son is crying again. Or is that me crying? I can't tell. I am wet, weak, and feverish. My son is running a fever too. Now he is coughing.*

"Mommy. I'm thirsty. I want water."

"I'm sorry baby. Not now. You have to wait for water."

"Mommy. I have to go to the bathroom."

"Can you hold it?"

"No. I have to go now!"

"Don't go now. I will take you up the ladder. Hold on." With her basket of drinking water and rice hanging from a strap on one shoulder, her purse inside the basket too, she squeezed her son to the side of her body. Lien climbed the wooden ladder. After ascending the few feet to the ceiling she pounded on the underside of the trap door and someone from the outside lifted it open.

The officious man with the whistle said, "Sorry lady, you must stay below. We have too many people up here already."

"My son has to go to the toilet. *Nha ve sinh o dau?* I have to go too."

He grabbed under her arms and pulled them up.

"Some have been going in this bucket." He pointed to a pail sitting on the deck, half full of urine.

She scowled at him.

He shrugged and said, "See that plank over there?" He pointed to the side of the ship where a one-foot wide board extended over the water. Attached to the end of the plank was a cubicle made of canvass to provide some privacy.

"That is the bathroom?"

"Yes," he said snidely. "It has all the comforts of your shit pond back home but a little breezier."

"Don't be afraid," she said to her son. "I will hold your hand and we will go together."

When they finished they carefully made their way back to the boat, thankful the sea was calm at that moment. Others were lined up on the deck waiting their turn to use the makeshift facility.

When they got back to the deck she let go of her son's hand and leaned against the bulkhead, enjoying the breezy mist, the sunshine, and the fresh air. It was crowded but livable on the deck. She pushed hair away from her face and took deep refreshing breaths.

A man who appeared to be in his seventies was leaning on the wall next to her. "I hope you are going to be all right down in that hold," he said.

"It's horrible. I think people are going to die down there. There is no air and it is very hot," she said.

"This is the second time I have done this," he volunteered.

"What do you mean?"

"I was one of the original Boat People. When the communist took over the North in 1954, I got on one of the boats and went south with a million other people. But I knew where I was going then. Now I'm on a boat again to flee the communist but this time I don't know where I'm going."

"I want to go to America," she said.

"Yes, don't we all? This time we don't get to choose. Somebody will decide for us, I suspect. I think the Vietnamese will be sent all over the world."

"Maybe the American Navy will take us to the United States."

"Maybe, but the Americans have left us. The ocean and the

wind might decide where we go, and then we might end up in some country that does not want us and they might send us back to the communists so they can work us to death," he said.

"I have to keep my dreams and my dream for my little boy."

"Is he American?"

"Yes. He's half American."

"It's good that you take him and give him a chance in life. He's a fine looking boy," he said and patted the shy child on the head.

"*Cam on,*"Lien said, noticing the old man had smooth hands, no calluses.

"We are the cap blowing off a dormant volcano, spewing fumes and lava to the four corners of the globe. We will become a fixture in many foreign lands. Any country that receives us will be fortunate because we are the ones who will fight and work hard for a better life. We are the ones too brave to stay and take orders."

"You're making me feel much better."

"I speak for you and your son; not for myself. I'm old and may not have much time to contribute to a new country. But I'm too stubborn to take orders from ignorant sheep. They would soon kill me one way or another."

"Sir, my name is Lien. What is your name?"

Whistle man approached again. "Hey lady, you can't stand around here taking up space. Go down the ladder where you belong. Then he opened the hatch for her.

"It was nice meeting you," she told the old man and started descending into the darkness, clutching her son.

He smiled at her. "I will talk to you later."

CHAPTER 27

"Dreams Are Not Free"

<u>South China Sea, 1976</u>

It was an agonizing night. The sea got rougher. The groaning of the old man under Lien's bench got even weaker. All around her people were suffering.

When shafts of illumination showed through the cracks in the overhead planks, Lien took her boy up on deck again to use the crude toilet. There was a long line for the one facility that jutted out from the side of the old fishing boat.

She did not mind waiting in line, anything to delay her return to the hot stench below deck. The breeze felt good. It was sunny but the day had not yet warmed. Lien watched some people dipping water from the ocean in an attempt to take a simple bath. Others had lines in the water trying to catch fish.

Lien overheard some men talking quietly about the detention camp they escaped. Another said he paid a large bribe to leave the country and now had nothing. A woman intervened to say she had to sell her everyday belongings piece by piece in order to survive. When she began sending her children to forage for food in garbage piles she knew it was time to leave Vietnam.

Lien had never heard her people talk so openly about their problems. Vietnamese usually kept their troubles to themselves, particularly after the communists took over. This talk, even though guarded in subdued tones, and obviously among friends, made her feel uncomfortable.

She moved away from them as much as possible while still keeping her place in line to use the toilet. The distinguished old man Lien had talked to the day before was nearby, leaning against the bulkhead again.

"*Chao co* (Hello young lady)" he said.

"*Chao bac* (Hello old man)" she replied and bowed slightly.

"I see you survived the night."

"Yes. I don't think anyone died yet."

"Not yet," he said. "The sea, once reminding people of peace and beauty, now becomes a symbol of darkness, violence, separation, and death."

The man's formal and descriptive speech raised her curiosity. *This is a strange but educated old man*, she thought. *Maybe he is a poet or a professor.*

"Where are we going?" she asked

"Away."

"Away to where?"

"Nobody knows. The rich and the middle-class were stripped of their homes, their jobs, and their belongings. The rich are now poor and the poor are now rich. So, we go away," he said, pulling on his gray beard, "but no one knows where."

"In my dreams I know where I am going."

"Even though we are free to dream, the dreams are not free," he said. "We all paid for our dreams and some also had to pay the government or local officials to dream. Nowhere else in the world does a government traffic in its own citizens. They are corrupt beyond imagination."

Lien looked around to see if anyone was listening to this dangerous conversation. She thought there might be spies on the boat. Lien did not know what to say. Her parents still had their home when she left. She worried about them.

"Don't worry, my child," the old man said. "What can they do to us now? I think the captain would sink the boat rather than be captured."

"Sir, I don't want to hear such talk. It scares me."

"Just think; when you survive this, nothing in your entire life will scare you again. Nothing can compare to this journey."

"If I had left last year, the U.S. Seventh Fleet would have been anchored here to rescue us but now they have gone."

"Look out to the sea. At a distance you see merchant ships, tugboats, fishing vessels, landing craft; all heading east. So many ships cannot be ignored."

"Yes, and they all look unseaworthy."

The old man laughed. "You cannot tell that from here. You must keep your dream. This is the great adventure of your life. It will shape you and your future and that of your beautiful blond haired boy."

Lien took her son's hand and moved up in line a little. The old man fascinated her and scared her. She wondered why he took such an interested in her. It seemed that he could almost read her mind.

The engine noise was much less distracting on deck. It was a relief and allowed her to hear the gossip and rumors that she could not hear below deck.

Lien saw a young man observing her.

He approached her with a smile, displaying a fine set of white teeth. "They call me 'Jade,'" he said.

"Hello," Lien said suspiciously. She did not offer her name. Lien did not believe this was his real name and wondered why he was hiding his identity.

"I was a college student," he offered, "but when the communist took over all the schools were closed, so I went home to the Mekong Delta."

Lien nodded.

"I soon found out that I was not welcome in my old village by the new leaders. They were uncomfortable to have an educated person in their midst to question their decisions. Soon they had me arrested for being disloyal."

Why is he telling me this? Lien wondered.

"So, I was sent to a work camp near the Cambodian border. My job was to destroy helicopter landing pads with an ax and sledge hammer to make room for a garden. We were fed very little, some rice in the morning and at night. I was so hungry I grabbed crickets and lizards and ate them raw when the guards were not looking. If they would've caught me eating, when I should have been working, they would have beaten me."

Lien grimaced.

"One night I was in luck. The Khmer Rouge crossed the border and attacked the camp. Many soldiers were wounded. I was ordered to help carry the camp commander to the medical station. When we stopped to rest I ran away in the dark and made my way back to my village."

"Obviously your escape was successful," Lien said.

"Yes, but my mother said I could not stay. She gave me some gold, which I used to travel to Vung Tau and to pay for passage on to this old fishing boat. If they catch me now I will be killed."

"Good luck; it was nice meeting you," Lien said, and moved up in line.

She assumed Jade had not been in the army for South Vietnam and wondered why a young healthy man like Jade had not served. *He was a draft dodger,* she thought.

Another passenger introduced himself. "Hello; my name is Dr. Tho. I was a physician," he said.

Why are all these people talking to me? Lien wondered. She looked around the boat. Everyone looked haggard, disheveled, beaten. *Maybe I am the best looking woman on the ship. My clothes are still relatively clean, I have tried to keep my appearance decent, and I certainly don't feel beaten. I have always been attractive and I still am. These men are as frightened as I am, so they want someone sympathetic to talk to.*

The physician remained at her side. "The new leaders did not like my education," he said. "I was soon sent to a reeducation camp where I pretended to be a model communist citizen. After my release I bought a small boat to peddle cabbages up and down the Saigon River. My friends thought I was crazy for not going back to being a doctor. They said I must have been tortured and therefore lost my mind. I let them think what they wanted but I got the communist guards to trust me. Since I was 'reformed' they allowed me to travel anywhere I wanted in my sampan. The night before last I put my entire family, instead of cabbages, on my boat and sailed right up to this fishing boat and climbed on aboard. I bet they're missing me now," he said with a laugh.

"We need doctors on the boat," Lien said.

"Yes, but I don't have any medicine or bandages with me. I will do what I can."

Lien and the doctor looked toward a disturbance on board. A distraught man was ranting and waving his arms.

"I should not be on this boat!" the man cried.

Everyone looked at him with shock.

"I don't know where my wife and children are! They were supposed to meet me here. When I got on the boat I thought maybe they had come here already, so I boarded the boat to look for them. I cannot find them! I left without them. They won't survive without me."

Dr. Tho ran to him. "We will help you look for them. What are their names and what is your name?"

He gave the gathering crowd his name and the name of his family members. Then he threatened to jump overboard.

The doctor said quietly to others, "Keep an eye on him."

Lien could not help but overhear the distraught man. "I was an ARVN officer," he said. "I fought for my country. I had money once. I was able to bribe my way out of a reeducation camp and three times I tried to escape with my family to America. Every time I paid for passage on a boat and every time I was cheated out of my money. I survived as a homeless person in Saigon and sometimes, I'm not proud to say, I had to live as an outlaw. Finally, I have paid for the escape again and the boat was there to take me and my family. But my wife and children might have been caught. How will I find them again?" He slumped to the deck and comforting hands patted him on the back.

"We will look for them," the doctor reassured.

"May I say something, gentleman?" someone said. A thin Buddhist monk with a creased face and wearing the traditional orange gown and headdress approached the gathering.

"I should have stayed to suffer with my people," he said quietly. "Maybe I am wrong to be here also."

Lien thought, *Not another confession. What is wrong with people? The stress of this trip is getting to people already. What will happen if we have to stay on this boat for a week or two?*

The holy man had now gathered a larger audience. "I lived much of my life being wrong. I always spoke for peace and reconciliation. I spoke for a negotiated settlement with the North. I criticized the Diem and Thieu regimes for ignoring me. Maybe I was too quick to criticize. When the northern soldiers came to my city I went out to greet them. In response they threatened me with their guns and one soldier hit me in the face with his rifle. Another soldier said there is no religion just before he shot and killed the priest standing next to me. Then they tore my temple apart, riddled the Buddha statue with bullets and slashed the alter cloths with bayonets. Next they pushed me into a corner and took turns urinating on me and laughing."

Everyone was silent for a moment. They had never heard a monk talk this way. No one knew what to say. Some of the men bowed to the monk. With his head down, the depressed man in orange ambled alone to the other end of the boat.

Lien began to realize she was much stronger than many of the passengers. Listening carefully and observing peoples' mannerism she recognized there were many professionals on her rickety fishing boat – politicians, teachers, store owners, and military officers. Many had lived privileged lives before they found themselves on this decrepit boat in the middle of the South China Sea.

One frail man claimed to be a heart surgeon. Another said

he was a schoolmaster. A man with dark skin and rough hands said he had repaired old boats so they could float again. This job, however, became too dangerous because the authorities were trying to stop such activity.

After Lien and her son returned from the toilet, she guided him toward the hatch leading to the ship's hold.

CHAPTER 28

"Going Away"

<u>South China Sea, 1976</u>

In the dank hold of the ship more and more people began coughing. The old man under Lien's bench moaned continuously but quietly now. Some of the babies stopped crying. Lien held her little boy on her lap as he sobbed feverishly from hunger and thirst and fear.

She estimated they had drunk two-thirds of their water and eaten a similar fraction of their rice. The rice had been lightly seasoned with *nuoc mam* but now it was beginning to have a stinging sensation too. She could not see it in the dark but suspected little black ants had infected the rice and added their own seasoning. It could not be helped; they would eat the rice anyway.

Toward the end of the third day she thought she could feel the ship turn southward. The boat's engine began making strange rough noises. This could not be a good sign, she thought, even though the diesel engine valiantly continued to chug along.

That night the engine suddenly stopped, out of fuel. The abrupt silence woke Lien from a fitful sleep. The quiet was quickly replaced by expressions of concern from the crowd. She yelled and asked what was happening. Others were yelling too, so no one answered her.

After a few moments the sound of the engine was replaced by the crashing of waves. The ceiling began dripping water with an ammonia scent onto the passengers below. The urine bucket had not been emptied over the side of the boat and now it had been tipped over.

Conditions suddenly changed. An ominous cracking resounded throughout the hold as the ship was buffeted to one side and then the other. Some of the passengers tried to stand and move toward the hatch.

It felt like the boat came to a dead stop only to be hurled through the air a second later. Then it slammed down onto the surface of the water. Next the sea over washed the fishing boat. Again and again the slow destruction of the watercraft was repeated.

Those who were not seated were slammed to the floor or onto someone else. Arguments and protest were voiced.

More water splashed from the ceiling. One man made it to the hatch and proclaimed the way to the deck was locked. His pronouncement was followed by screams and protests.

"We are all going to drown!" someone exclaimed.

People rushed and crawled over each other. Lien surrounded her boy's body with hers. She fought to maintain her position on the bench while people landed on her back, stepped on her feet, and slammed their elbows and knees into the side of her head. She grimaced and defiantly held her position to protect her son.

The storm, in the dark, lasted for hours. The crushing, the water saturated air, and the panic made breathing difficult. Lien stubbornly resisted beckoning death. She had to live so her son could live.

It was a long night of turbulence. Without a working engine, the ship and its passengers were tossed about at the mercy of the sea. Lien could no longer tell what direction they were heading, nobody could.

As suddenly as it started, the storm began to subside.

Passengers crawled in filthy water in search of family members.

The starving people had expended their energy and tried to return to their original seats in a state of exhaustion, confusion, frustration. Some cried. Some prayed. Some would protest no more because they had been trampled to death or drowned. Life sustaining oxygen in the dark dungeon was now even more depleted.

Lien began to think that maybe she was fortunate. Many of those on deck were directly subjected to the elements and undoubtedly swept overboard to their death.

The night was endless. People were retching. Some were bleeding or suffering from broken bones. She could feel bruises on her own body.

"Mister," she yelled to the passenger who had claimed his spot under her bench. "Are you all right?"

There was no response. She yelled at him again. Nothing. "I did not even know your name," she said.

Lien touched her boy all over. "Are you all right? Are you hurt?"

"I'm hungry, Mommy."

"We will have to wait before we can eat again," she said, making sure she was still in possession of her jar of water and her metal can of cooked rice.

"Mommy, I'm so hungry."

"I know darling. Someday we will have all the food you can eat. Look, it's getting light again outside. Look at the ceiling and you can see light. And the sea is getting calmer. In another hour maybe we can go up on deck again."

"Mommy, I'm hot and tired and hungry."

"Yes, we all are. Can you feel that? The wind has died down and the water is calmer. We lived through the storm and our new home is closer."

"What new home? Where are we going?" he asked.

"You will see. Now be quiet and rest awhile." She had no idea where they were going.

Once on deck everyone had the same question. "Where are we going?"

Someone estimated they were drifting south.

Men who were strong enough volunteered to recover those who had died the night before. Most of the dead came from the ship's hold. Each body was slipped into the ocean while a Catholic priest and the Buddhist monk presided. Family members cried for their loved ones while others on deck appeared sullen and trance like.

"*Chao co*," the dignified old man said to Lien.

Lien turned quickly, and there he was, nearly in the same spot. "I was worried about you," she said.

"*Cam on*," he said. "I did not think anybody cared."

Feeling like he was the only friend she had on board, Lien said, "Well, I care about you. How did you survive the night?"

"I tied myself to a post and tried to get as low to the deck as possible. I almost drowned anyway. It was a very long bath."

"Do you know where we are going yet?"

"I told you. We are going away."

"What direction?"

"Someone said we are drifting south. I agree with that. You can ask the captain. He would have a compass. If we continue to float this slowly, however, we will never reach land before we die. And if we see another boat, they may be Thai pirates and they will kill us."

"I'm sorry I asked."

"I'm sorry I answered. Let's just say we are going 'away.'"

CHAPTER 29
"Rape, Murder, Pillage"

South China Sea, 1976

After the storm, with fewer surviving passengers, those who had been relegated to the hold of the ship were now allowed more hours on the sun splashed deck. Every night, however, they were required to return to their watery dungeon.

As the weather got hotter, some of the refugees on deck sprawled in what little shade they could find and slipped into semi-consciousness.

A gentle breeze continued to push the ship southward. Some enterprising young men gathered sheets and blankets to create a crude sail to propel them at a slightly faster pace.

Others gathered pieces of old rope to stuff into the cracks in the boat below the waterline. The seepage was reduced but not stopped.

Another group organized to bail out the seeping water using a variety of makeshift containers. As long as they continued their toil the boat was assured of staying afloat. Eventually the bailers formed two shifts, each working four hours on and four hours off, day and night.

Fresh water was depleted. Increasingly the refugees discretely collected their own urine and with disgust, drank some. Termites were dug out of the wood to eat or use for fishing bait. What leather they could find was soaked, cut into tiny pieces, chewed and eventually swallowed.

Lien overheard a small group of tough-looking men gather to discuss the dangers of sailing into the lawless area east of Thailand.

"Should we scare our people by preparing to fight the Thai pirates?" one man asked.

"Rumors of the pirates have already spread throughout the ship," another man said. "Have you ever heard of the term 'RMP'?"

"No."

In English it means 'rape, murder, pillage.' If we are unlucky, that is what we can expect."

A dark skinned man who looked like a fisherman said, "Our worst enemy used to be the North Vietnamese Navy, but now it's the Thai pirates. Most of them were fishermen and know these waters. Robbing us is easier than catching fish. They're becoming more and more bold, sometimes even entering Vietnam waters. A few years ago the pirates would simply board boats and take valuables. But now they fight each other too, leaving only the most vicious to continue their piracy."

The ship captain unexpectedly joined the group. They all looked at him, wondering what he would say. "Don't let me discourage you from talking about this." He paused for a moment, and then continued. "Now that our engine has stopped, we could be at the mercy of people who have no mercy. Boat People might not be welcome in other countries because there is starting to be too many of us. Piracy is out of control partly because no one wants to save us. I heard about one captain who sank his boat when the Thai Navy tried to pull his boatload of people back to the ocean where the pirates were waiting. I would do the same. I would rather risk drowning or being put into a Thai prison, than being sent to the pirates."

The group of discouraged looking men shuffled their feet and looked down at the deck.

"Let me tell you something I learned from another ship captain," he continued. "The pirates have gotten organized and have formed competing gangs. A favorite strategy is to form circles of eight or ten boats and whenever a refugee vessel enters the circle, they all converge on the hapless victim. All the boats in the raid share in the loot and fight off any other boats not part of their circle. These circles are about five to ten kilometers across and once you get into this trap there is no escape."

"Captain, what are they going to steal? We have nothing."

"As long as you have the clothes on your back, you have something to steal. I know some of you have much more than that."

"Captain, will all or our young women be raped?"

"That's what usually happens, gang rape. It can go on for hours, even days. And right out in the open."

More head shaking followed. "Vietnamese would never do that," someone said.

"Yes and the Thais think they are superior to us," the captain scoffed. "Then they have to cover up the evidence of their crimes. I have heard of everyone on a boat being beheaded, shot, stabbed or clubbed to death before being thrown overboard. All their possessions are stolen. Then the boat is rammed and sunk. Sometimes people survive such an attack but they are never the same again."

"Captain, for the most part we are unarmed, we are

carrying our savings in order to start a new life and we are unprotected. What can we do?"

"We should pray," someone yelled.

Some scoffed at that suggestion.

"Our boat is just floating out in the middle of the ocean. We can't do anything!" another exclaimed.

"Gentlemen," the captain said. "First and foremost, I need your cooperation and leadership. It is true that there isn't a lot we can do. But we can be courageous and not allow others to panic. The pirates don't find every boat escaping Vietnam. It's a big ocean. We might be lucky."

One composed looking gentleman, standing in the back who had not participated in the conversation, raised his hand, "Captain, the ancient Chinese manuscript written by Sun-tzu named 'The Art of War,' advises that when you are weak you must look strong."

"That's good advice," the captain said. "If we look helpless and defeated we only invite being attacked. Much of what we have been talking about must be shared with everyone. Most important, we don't want to be caught by surprise. Please help me in gathering everyone who is able to come to the deck in front of my cabin in the next half hour. We can give advice to everyone on my boat to stand together and be brave."

The captain walked away and the others exchanged ideas for a few more minutes, and then returned to their part of the boat in order to organize the gathering for the captain.

Lien found her old friend and told him about the meeting.

"Yes, we need to go to the meeting. We need to hear what

he has to say."

Everyone on the boat who could move came to the assembly. Out of weariness most sat on the deck, some leaned on canes.

The captain loudly cleared his throat. "Thank you. You have all placed your trust in me and I'm doing my best to bring you to your new life in safety. This has been very hard on everyone and I'm sorry for those who have lost loved ones.

"As you know, we are going to continue south. We have no choice. This is the way the wind is blowing us. South is the closest way to a refugee camp but it is also going to take us through the area where the Thai pirates operate. This cannot be helped."

Mumbles of concern spread through the crowd.

"It's possible that we could fix the engine. It got flooded by the sea but that is not why it stopped. We simply ran out of fuel. As you know, diesel is scarce and I bought as much fuel as I could. We have no diesel now, but I know a couple of you hid cooking stoves on the boat. Now you have nothing to cook. With the fuel from your stove we could use it in an emergency for a short distance. Bring it to me.

"If any of you have weapons to protect us, like guns or knives or long sticks, or even hoes and rakes, then get ready to use them. If the pirates catch us, we might as well fight back, because they will try to kill everyone. I have heard that we cannot try to surrender because they will kill us anyway."

Some of the women began crying.

"I'm not trying to scare you. I want you to know what we can expect if the pirates try to stop us. We may not be able to tell which boat is a pirate ship and which is not. So, I say we won't ask any ship we see for help unless it is from a national navy or if it is flying a flag of the United States, Great Britain, France or Germany. I've heard they are willing to help us. I think Hong Kong and Australia will help us too. But if it is a fishing boat we will have to look like we can resist. Point your sticks and knives in their direction and say nothing. From a distance the sticks may look like rifles.

"We also have ropes we can throw into the water in front of pirate ships. If they run over the ropes it might foul their propellers so they can't chase us.

"Also, I hate to say this, women are in particular danger. I suggest you darken your skin, if you can. If you look dark they might not think you are Vietnamese. I don't know if this will work but we need to try everything."

More women began crying. The men looked grim, some trying to comfort the women.

"If we are lucky enough to get some rain, we will need to catch as much of it as we can. I need some volunteers to figure out how we can catch the rain so we have water to drink. We have some rain barrels on board but they are dry. Who can work on this project?"

Seven men and two women raised their hands.

"Thank you. You people get together and figure out how we can do this. I also have two buckets and some plastic sheeting you can have to catch water. Come see me afterward.

"Are there any questions? Is there anything else I should talk about?"

One man raised his hand and asked, "Captain. What country are we trying to get to?"

"I would like to go to Malaysia, but if we miss that,

Indonesia. I understand they are set up to take refugees. I don't think we can trust Thailand or Cambodia, although they have refugee camps too. Australia would take us but I think we won't survive that long. It's too far away. Since we're going south the Philippines and Hong Kong are out of the question. It is possible that an American or British ship could take all of us. But keep in mind; I have little means of steering this boat. We will probably go until we hit something or another boat pulls us to shore.

"Any other questions?"

There followed a lot of mumbling by the worried passengers. Then one man raised his hand and the captain nodded at him.

"I was a military officer, Captain. I would like to organize our defense."

The ship captain nodded at him again. "Yes, what is your name?"

"Just call me Colonel."

"Colonel, what are your ideas?"

"I would like everyone with a weapon to meet me here in an hour. In the meantime, if you have a rake or hoe or long stick, sharpen one end of it to make a pike.

"If you have a gun, now is the time to clean it. If you have a knife, now is the time to sharpen it, if you can. Then, everyone meet right here in one hour and we will see how many weapons we have and how much ammunition. We can practice how we will organize to defend ourselves."

Some of the passengers clapped their hands.

The captain said, "Did you hear that? Everyone who is able, meet with the colonel right here and we will practice to protect ourselves.

"I also want to thank those who have taken it upon themselves to plug the leaks in the boat and those who are continuing to bail out the water. Please keep doing this work. You are keeping us afloat.

"Another thing, all lights must be out after dark. We have to run at night in complete darkness and silence. My family members will keep watch at night and warn you of any trouble.

"As said before, this is a good time to sharpen your sticks or hoes or pruning hooks, or whatever you can turn into a weapon. If you have a gun, then it is the time to clean it. We are entering the most dangerous part of our trip.

"Again, if you have any fuel, see me in my cabin."

The captain, his voice now dry and hoarse, walked away and climbed to his cabin. Most passengers walked with their families to the area of the boat they called their own, their spirits a little brighter. Others, with little strength left, stayed right where they were seated.

Thirst, hunger, and the Thai pirates were on everyone's mind.

CHAPTER 30

What now?

That night the wind increased again, still blowing them south. Lien held onto her boy firmly, although he was now too weak to struggle. The filthy water sloshed around her feet as the boat rocked side to side. In the darkness the bailers continued their work throughout the night.

From his perch the captain and his family scanned the ocean with binoculars for danger in the form of other ships, floating debris, and land. Ship lights were seen in the distance while the captain maintained lights out and reached for his rifle.

Those who were encamped on deck suffered from sun and wind burn. And now the turbulence again. Constant exposure to the elements brought fatigue, dehydration and clothing encrusted with dried perspiration. They were no longer sweating, however. Their skin was feverish and itching and painful. Their limbs and head ached. Those who had once been strong were now weak.

The dwellers below deck fared no better. Many were nauseous even though their stomachs were empty. They suffered from irritating skin rashes and had persistent coughs. Lien wondered how long any of them could last. She tried to count the days they had been aboard – about a week she thought. Food and water had run out three days ago. She and her boy, Vinh, had not been to the toilet in two days; there was no need.

Somehow, so far, they avoided the vicious Thai pirates.

The wind got stronger, buffeting the boat, making it difficult for the bailers to keep their balance. The hull of the boat began creaking and groaning again. Those caulking the cracks worked feverishly by flickering candlelight.

Lien contemplated her death. There was so much she wanted to do in life and felt that she had accomplished little. If her Vinh died in her arms she would believe her life to have been a failure. By nature, she had been an optimistic person but she felt herself losing hope. The fatigue, the dizziness she felt, the pain in her joints, neck, back, made it difficult to think about anything except fighting to retain her balance on the hard narrow bench.

Each sound below deck seemed to compete for prominence: the jarring, groaning, grating of the planks that might become their coffin. The sloshing, swishing, gurgling that might drown them. The coughing, moaning, murmuring of her agony, or from someone else, she could not tell anymore.

The rocking increased. Their speed increased too, she thought, but it could be her imagination. She no longer trusted her own thoughts.

What was real? Maybe this was what it was like to die. If she yelled maybe no one would hear her because she was already dead. Or maybe, just no one would care. Or, no one would hear because she was the only one left alive. She did not know and was not sure if she cared.

Her son cried out hoarsely, crying in his sleep. *I must live for him. I cannot give up.*

The next day continued the same. It was too dangerous to go topside. She fought endlessly to maintain her position on the wooden bench, to hold onto Vinh, to keep breathing the foul air. The agony was relentless. She fell asleep and dreamed she was dying.

With her heart pounding, gasping for breath, she was unexpectedly alert again, which meant her senses were more aware of her pain, dizziness, weakness, uncertainty. How much time had elapsed? She did not know but could see it was nighttime again.

The boat slammed, jolted, knocking her off the bench into the bilge water. Seawater poured through the sides of the boat.

The boat is falling apart. We are going to drown.

She grabbed her son who was now screaming. Others were screaming too. In the dark she stumbled toward the short ladder that led to the deck. The hatch was open; water poured down on her. To her surprise no one was blocking the exit. *Get out, get out!*

With the boat tilting increasingly to the side, she awkwardly climbed the ladder while grasping her son to her side. Once on deck she slid toward the outside railing. In the dark she saw the silhouette of a forest beyond a shoreline.

She climbed over the railing, still holding her son, and bravely jumped into the water. At first the water was up to her neck. Vinh clambered to her shoulders. She trudged forward in the foaming surf; fighting the resistance of the sand and water. She looked around and saw others doing the same. The more she marched, the shallower the water. When she reached the beach she ran and stumbled for fifty yards, then exhausted, she dropped to the sand, still holding her son.

She sat there a moment, catching her breath. "We are alive," she gasped. She sobbed.

They lay there, clutching each other, throughout the night. It was somewhat like sleeping but Lien was not sure. The crashing of the waves throughout the night, the mutter of other survivors, an occasional flicker of light, disrupted her tenuous sleep. Her hunger and thirst were unrelenting.

When the dawn came she rubbed her eyes and tried to brush the sand off her arms and legs. The damp grit only scratched her tender skin. Sand fleas attacked them at night, adding to their discomfort.

The thought of the Thai pirates surged back to mind. She could not lie on the beach if she wanted to protect herself and her child. She looked around and saw the treeline a short distance away. It looked dark green and cool.

Where are we? On a small island, I think. I wonder what country this is.

At sunrise the natural cacophony of an orchestra tuning up emitted from the jungle. Lien grabbed her son and staggered toward the dense foliation for safety and maybe water and something to eat. She found others hiding in the forest also.

The trees were so densely packed that Lien sometimes had to turn sideways and pull her son behind to squeeze between them. Vines looped around the trunks and hung from limbs to slow their progress. *A machete would come in handy now*, Lien thought.

Insects buzzed around them, getting in their hair, ears and nostrils. Above them, from the canopy, squawks resounded from unseen birds to warn the animal kingdom that intruders were approaching.

Lien struggled as the landscape titled upward. As it got steeper, the vegetation thinned slightly. She saw a clump of bananas. And moved upward them.

The bananas were small and sweet but Lien and her son could not swallow the nourishing fruit. Their throats were simply too dry. They held the paste in their mouths hoping saliva would come. They picked more bananas and stuffed them into their pockets and moved still higher.

When they reached what was initially believed to be the summit of a small hill, they looked across the terrain and saw the southern shore of the tiny island. Looking down Lien quickly realized they were on the edge of a bowl and at the bottom of the depression was water. The island was an extinct volcano with a caldera filled with fresh water.

She made this discovery on her own. No one else had explored this far inland. She was now convinced she and her son would live.

"Vinh, hold my hand," she said. "See the water? We are going down there."

They made their way downhill toward the water, sometimes sliding, sometimes stumbling in the volcanic ash toward the water filled caldera. When they got to the blue water they fell on their knees and drank. Nothing ever tasted so good or refreshing.

When Lien and her son drank their fill she carefully tested the depth of the little lake near its shore. It was shallow and cool. It was inviting and made her laugh.

They waded in up to her knees and then sat down on the sandy bottom. It was like heaven. They took the fine grain sand

and delicately rubbed themselves, cleaning their arms and legs. Oil from their skin made little rainbow splotches on the surface of the still water.

Next they splashed water on their faces, under their arms, their private places, and then they dunked their heads and scrubbed their hair. Lien was normally a very clean person; she hated even going a day without a bath. The soapless bath was not adequate but it was very welcome nonetheless. Vinh grinned and splashed her and she splashed him back. It made Lien's heart thump to see her son smile for the first time in a week.

Lien looked around and still saw no one. She grabbed the bananas they had left on shore. "Now we are going to eat the bananas," she said. The first they ate rapidly, the second and third more slowly. Although the bananas were small, they felt stuffed.

After a few minutes of relaxing, Lien said, "Now we are going to wash our clothes." She slipped off her clothes under water and her son did the same. They squished and beat them between their hands, then submersed them again, found a big rock at the shoreline and beat them some more. Then they rinsed and rang out the clothes, stepped from the lake, and put them on.

"We'll sit here awhile and let the sun dry us," she said.

She noticed that the water, despite all of their activity, was not muddy. It remained clear because there was no soil sediment, only sand in the bottom of the little lake. It was very much unlike the fresh water she knew in Vietnam, which was always very turbid.

Refreshed but still very tired, Lien began to wonder what

was next. *Where are we going to sleep tonight? And what else are we going to eat? We just can't eat bananas. This lake looks too clear to support fish.*

And where is everybody? Maybe they are being rescued now and we are being left behind. Or maybe something horrible has happened to them. Were they all killed or kidnapped?

As she sat on the shore, her knees drawn up to her chest, and her arms around her knees, she felt a little shiver of uncertainty.

What now?

CHAPTER 31

"Basket Full of Knowledge"

Unnamed island, Indonesia, 1976

They slept fitfully at the edge of the small clear lake. By dawn they were fully awake.

"Vinh, we can't stay," Lien said. "No one will rescue us here. Nobody knows we're here. They'll probably think we drowned in the ocean. I don't know what we will find but we have to go back."

"Yes, mother. I want to go home."

"I told you before. We're going to a new home, not our old home."

Tears came to Vinh's eyes. "I just want to go home. I want to see grandmother and grandfather."

She put her arm around him. "Drink some water from the lake and we will go to the beach."

The loose sand in the inter walls of the extinct volcano made climbing difficult. When they made it to the rim they stopped and rested, looking down at the little lake that saved them from thirst and brought comfort. To the north, above the treetops, they could barely see the shoreline of the island. Their ship and fellow passengers were not visible from their vantage point.

"I hope they haven't left us," Lien said, and then sorry she said anything, not wanting to frighten Vinh.

He did not seem to notice. His eyes were following a beautiful butterfly.

She took his hand and stepped into the woods. An hour later, with more bug bites and scratches, they emerged from the jungle to the sandy beach.

First, Lien saw the damaged fishing boat on its side at the surf line being buffeted by the waves. Next, she saw some people milling about it, apparently trying to salvage items from inside the wreck. A couple sailors, holding rifles, stood nearby, not helping them but not harassing them either.

Most of her former shipmates were missing. *What happened to them?* she wondered. *I don't know if it is safe here.*

Then she saw her old friend from the fishing boat standing near the edge of the jungle. He was thinner and frailer than ever. His clothes now hung from him in rags, but he continued to uphold a certain amount of dignity as he leaned on a walking stick far from the other people.

Lien walked to him.

His bedraggled appearance was shocking but he spoke first. "Lien, I was worried about you and your boy."

"I was worried about you; now you are worrying about us," Lien said.

He laughed. "Well, God cannot seem to kill us."

"Where is everybody? Where have they gone?"

"They were rescued yesterday by the Indonesian Navy. They could not take everyone in their small ship. They said they would be back today. When today, I don't know."

"Where are they taking us?" Lien asked.

"They said there are two refugee camps, one named Galang I and the other named Galang II. How creative of them. And it's on Galang Island, which is a big island, I heard. That's all I know. They seemed nice, kind of stern, like all military. They brought water but no food, so everyone is still hungry."

"What are people doing with the fishing boat?"

"Some people have their savings and valuables in the boat. They are still trying to find them, so they refused to go on the first rescue ship."

"That's what I thought. Yes, I still have my valuables on board too," Lien joked. "A tin can and a glass jar."

"You kept your spirit. That's how you survived," he said with a smile.

"I've been able to hold onto my plastic satchel and purse inside too. How did _you_ survive?" she asked.

"I survive by accepting my fate," he said. "Don't fight nature. The wind blew me here and I accept it. Whatever happens next, I will allow it to happen."

"Are you Buddhist?"

"In culture, but not in religion. Reason is my religion."

"I was raised as a Buddhist but my father is Catholic."

"Maybe you should be Catholic for this venture. A Western country would be more likely to take you in."

"I had not thought of that. Well, since we are allowing fate to determine our destiny," Lien said, "I'm just sitting down here on this rock and allowing myself to be rescued."

"May I sit with you?" he asked.

"Certainly," she said.

The old man struggled to sit down next to her. "Your son is one of the _con lai_ (half-breeds), am I right?

"You asked me that before."

"I'm getting old and forgetful."

"Yes, he's half American. Thank you for not calling him *bui doi* (the dust of life)."

"He is fortunate to have a good mother. Sometimes mixed race children are abandoned by both their father and their mother."

"I could never do that," Lien said. "He's a good boy and smart. I escaped Vietnam partly for him. He is teased mercilessly by other children. Even adults avoid contact with him because somehow they would become tainted. Some people are so stupid and cruel. His grandmother would die his hair so he would look more Vietnamese. I think under these conditions, where nearly everyone discriminated against him, he would become mean. He's not mean yet but sometimes very confused. He deserves to have a good life and not be punished for my mistakes."

"I knew you were a good mother," he said. "If you stayed in Vietnam he would now also be considered a 'child of the enemy.'"

"Yes, you are right."

"Things would be even worse for him under the communists," the old man said.

"You are so smart."

"I try to be but sometimes I fail. It wasn't smart to come on this journey. I'm old and will die soon, yet I'm here taking food and space away from those who deserve to live a long and healthy life, like you and your son."

"Don't say that," Lien said. "You still have many years ahead of you and you must teach the younger ones how to live."

"I feel like you are a daughter to me," he said.

"And my son is your grandson," she said.

"You are too kind."

"I think I see a ship coming," Lien said and stood.

"Wait. Stay here by the jungle's edge. We don't know who they are yet."

Lien shaded the sun from her eyes with her hand. "The ship is painted gray. It's too big to come closer, I think. They are lowering three smaller boats into the water."

"What are they doing now?"

"It looks like the smaller boats are coming to the island."

"Can you see the flag on the ship?" the old man asked.

"Yes. It is red and white, I think."

"Are you sure?"

"Yes. I see it better now. It's red on the top and white below."

"Then get ready to go. They will take you to Galang Island."

"What do you mean? You are going too."

"I will walk you to the surf."

"Can I help you?"

"No thank you, *Chau*. I found this fine stick to help me walk."

They moved slowly to the beach. Others ran to the surf, wanting to be the first on a rescue boat. Some were frantic, still looking for their lost valuables.

The guards on the beach made people get into three orderly lines to board the boats.

As the boats came closer, some of the refugees shouted with excitement but most were too weak to show any emotion, using the last bit of their strength just to stand in line.

"This will be the last rescue effort from this island," one of the navy guards shouted in his native language, but none of the Vietnamese understood him. "Everyone must get in one of the three boats to take you to our ship." Then he physically pushed people around to assure the same number of people in each line.

Lien held her boy close to her so they would not be separated.

"Those in the left line will get on the boat on the left. Those in the center line will get on the boat in the middle. Those in line on the right will get on the boat on the right. There will be no changing lines. You are all going to the ship. So if your family is split up, don't worry about it. You're all going to meet up on the ship."

The motor boats came within two yards of the beach, their engines throttled down and facing the land.

"Now everyone get on board. No pushing."

The refugees waded into the warm surf, some helping others to get onto the bobbing boats.

Lien looked behind her. "Old man, where're you going? Why are you walking away?"

"I'm going to let nature decide what to do with me. The refugee camp will be hard. I won't take food out of your mouths," he said as he turned and walked toward the jungle.

A guard pushed Lien toward the boat with his rifle. "Move lady, you're holding everyone up."

"The old man is walking in the wrong direction." She pointed to him.

"Sir, one of them is getting away," the guard shouted to his commanding officer.

"Maybe the old fool wants to stay here on this deserted island," was his response. "We don't have time to chase down every crazy Vietnamese. The fewer of them the better."

The guard then turned to Lien, pushing her again. "Now move it or you will be left too."

With tears in her eyes, holding her son, Lien boarded the boat.

The old man continued to hobble toward the jungle and did not look back.

Once everyone was on board, the powerful motor boats surged toward the mother ship and away from the small isolated island and the old gentleman.

Once on the navy ship Lien joined others holding onto the outside railing. *At least I don't have to go below with the rats and the stench and the heat.* Vinh held her around the waist and look stunned.

The wind blew her hair and her blouse. It was refreshing. She felt something in her blouse pocket, a piece of paper; she pulled it out to read:

"*Di mot ngay dang, hoc mot sang khon.* (Go out one day and come back with a basket full of knowledge.)"

Below that was the address and phone number of a professor in Boston. "Contact my friend who can help you find the basket," it said.

CHAPTER 32

Galang I

Galang, Indonesia, 1976

The wooden dock undulated under their feet as Lien gripped Vinh's hand. They stood in line with a hundred other Boat People. The officials looked confused. Indonesian Navy guards stood at the perimeter of the large dock with their rifles over their arm. Men donning police uniforms bustled frantically, giving each other orders in a language the refugees did not understand.

Hot breeze blew from the ocean, the dock swayed with the incoming waves and whenever the weakened refugees tried to sit down the armed sailors ordered them to stand. The beach front on both sides of the dock was lined with stores and houses on stilts. Naked children swam near the dock to get a closer look. The local adult residents scowled at them, the disruptors of their tranquility.

The refugees, who had not eaten in days, became dizzy, some fainting, and others sitting down regardless of the protests from the sailors. The bedraggled newcomers begged for water and food but their pleas were ignored.

In the distance they could hear the faint pounding of carpenters and the sound of machinery.

After an hour or two some large white men and women wearing "UN" on their blue shirts told them in poor Vietnamese to line single file and walk about two kilometers straight ahead to their camp. The young helped the sick and elderly struggle forward.

When they walked through the village the local residents gawked at them and yelled unintelligible insults.

When they entered the gates of "Galang I" they saw a camp still under construction. Many barracks style buildings were nearing completion. That was when Lien realized they were some of the first to occupy the camp.

Those who arrived even earlier were industriously planning a café, a fruit stand, a grocery store, and a movie theater. Lien felt even poorer, realizing she had no money to afford the services these new businesses had to offer.

At the makeshift village they were lined up again, this time before a large table with three clerks demanding to see identification and asking questions. Once through the registration process Lien and Vinh were assigned living quarters and to her surprise, handed a basket with eggs, green beans, rice, flour, and sugar.

They were lodged in a large shelter with 50 other people. Wide benches that stretched from one end of a long room to the other served as sleeping pallets. After showering, Lien and Vinh slept on their portion of the bench for a very long time.

They woke at dawn the next morning to the sounds of hammering, sawing, and chopping. Lien looked outside to see more buildings being constructed and men and women cultivating a community garden.

For the next few weeks more and more Boat People arrived but very few left. Lien was fearful that she and Vinh would never leave the place. She did not escape Vietnam to live in a commune, she told herself. She also did not battle the sea, starvation and uncertainty just to become idle.

Lien volunteered at a free lending library where books were available in Vietnamese, English, French and a few other languages. She also worked part-time in the café where she made a little money and was given food. Near her barracks she worked in the community garden. She also made sure Vinh went to the camp school six days a week.

Lien was told that the relocation process was long and uncertain. Those who fled for political and religious persecution were given priority. Leaving Vietnam simply for economic reasons alone was not a valid reason for relocation.

After another month Lien was carefully interviewed by a UN official. She told the agent she was married to an American Army officer and showed him her battered cohabitation permit with her picture and that of Captain Clint McGregor. She also said she was Catholic and that the communists were persecuting Catholics. Her son was discriminated against because he was half American.

"A cohabitation permit is not a marriage license," the stern looking UN worker stated.

"Crint have American wife; me his Vietnamee wife. Me full time wife to him."

"It's not the same," he said.

"Yes, it be same. He no pay me. You ask Crint," she said.

Filling out a form in front of her he said, "Ahuh, ahuh. Well, we can't do that right now. And you say you are Catholic?"

"Yes," and she showed him the cross hanging from her neck, the one she borrowed from another resident.

"And you have been subjected to religious persecution?"

Remembering the correct answer to that question, she simply said, "Yes."

"What are your volunteer activities at the camp?"

"I work garden," she said, attempting to speak clear English. "We grow squash now; you like?"

"Yes, next time we have a meeting I would like to have some of your squash," he said.

"I bring now."

"No, that won't be necessary."

"I work library, sew clothes, clean cabin, sweep ground outside."

"And your relatives outside of Vietnam?"

"I have cousins in Boston."

"In the United States?"

"Yes, in United States."

"And the person you call your husband, where is he?"

"He live Oregon. I try to find him."

"You speak English fairly well. I think with a little training you could speak perfect English."

"Yes?" She blushed. "Husband help me."

"Do you have a mailing address for your relatives in Boston?"

"Yes. I write."

He handed her a sheet of typing paper and a pencil.

She rapidly wrote down the address from memory and handed it back to him.

"You have good handwriting. Maybe you could help us in the office."

"I go high school in An Giang. I know professor in Boston."

He looked at the handwritten address and smiled. "So

you have contacts in Oregon and Boston. And you have been subjected to religious persecution. If you would have stayed in Vietnam you would have been subjected to political persecution too.

"Do you think you could interpret for us?"

"Maybe."

"Well, this is something we can talk about later. As you can see, we are still getting organized around here. This is a tough place and it's not going to get any better I'm afraid. Refugees are coming into this camp faster than they can be processed. Eventually we will be built up to handle 5,000 people but we are expecting 20,000 before we start placing people in other countries. We will need people like you to help us."

"I want to go America, not stay here work," she said.

"Lien, I understand. We won't keep you any longer than we have to. Our job is to determine whether you qualify to live in another country. Then we will send you there, if they want you, as soon as possible."

"And I no, what you say, qualify?"

"We would have to send you back to Vietnam if you don't qualify."

"Oh, Mister, please no do that," she said with tears glistening in her eyes.

"Lien, you already have good connections with the United States, you will probably qualify for political persecution, you have some education, and you don't appear to have a criminal record. I don't see any reason at this time why you would not qualify. But these things take time," he said.

"And Vinh, my boy?"

"He is a minor, so he would go where you go. In the

meantime, we are issuing identification cards. Here is yours. It is signed by me and you must sign on this line." He pointed to the space on the back of the card.

She nervously signed with the pen he handed her.

"You must keep this card with you at all times and show it whenever an official or guard asks to see it. Eventually, when we get better organized, we plan to issue cards with your picture on it.

"Now, let me caution you. Do not go anywhere at night. Do not leave the camp without permission. Stay away from the village. They hate you and they don't want you here. Do not try to help anyone escape. You can only go to the beach on Sunday but you will only go as an organized group. If anyone asks you for a bribe I want you to tell me or a member of our staff. You will be much better off if you do not talk to the Indonesian soldiers or officials here. You are an attractive woman and they will look at you and say things to you; just ignore them. Do you understand me?"

"Yes, sir."

"Good. If anything new happens on your case, one of us will let you know."

She stood and said, "Thank you, sir."

With a mechanical smile he looked at her and said, "Good luck."

She bowed and passed the next person being lead into the sparse office.

Lien retreated to her portion of the large room in her barracks, which was now walled off with some curtains for privacy. She lay down on the bench, exhausted and nervous from the meeting to determine her future. Vinh was still in school.

She decided that, on the next day, when she was more relaxed, she would write a letter to her cousin in Boston with the help of a woman in her barracks who worked for the Americans as a secretary. It took her three days to write and send the letter.

Dear Cousin,

My son Vinh and I are at Camp Galang I on an island in northern Indonesia. I believe it is just south of Singapore. We have been here for two months.

Many Vietnamese and some Cambodians and Laotians are coming here every day. It is a sad place. We risked our lives to come here for a better life but now we are in prison. Everyone wants to leave here for a better life. I fear that many of us will be sent back to Vietnam where we will be in an even worse prison.

I gave your name as someone who might sponsor us in the United States. You can help Vinh and I if you say you would welcome us to America.

We have no money, so our diet is very bad. If I had some money I could buy some fruit and fresh fish at the little market here. If you can send us some money I will pay you back when I find a job in America. A bank draft is no good here but everyone accepts American currency. Just please send money in a letter. They do not search our mail here. I am sorry I have to beg. Every two weeks we are given rice, canned fish, cooking oil and salt. If we had money we could buy seeds to grow our

own vegetables.

Each Saturday everybody is required to clean the street and their room. Only on Sunday we are allowed to go to the seashore, which is about two kilometers away.

It is not safe here and I do not want Vinh to grow up like a prisoner but he seems happy so far. He goes to school all day but they have no books. He has made friends with other American-Vietnamese boys. I make sure he does not wander off the camp like some of the older boys and get into trouble.

Someday I will tell you about the boat trips that brought us to this camp. Many on my ship died before we wrecked on a small island and then the Indonesian Navy brought us to this island. Vinh and I were strong enough to survive two storms at sea and no food or water for four days.

Although a Catholic Church, two Buddhist temples and two pubs were recently built here many cannot stand it here. Some people have committed suicide. I feel bad for them because they now cannot go to heaven.

One orphan girl I met was excited about being relocated to somewhere in Europe. A few days later she was told that the decision had been reversed. She was so distraught that she set herself on fire and died.

One night I heard screams in the camp. The next day I learned that six Vietnamese women had been raped by a gang of Vietnamese men. The next day all the women took their own lives.

Some men are so depressed at not having a job to support their family that they throw themselves into a ravine and die.

I heard about one area of the camp where no one else can go. It is isolated for those who ate human flesh of those who died when they were at sea and starving. On our boat when people died they were buried at sea. No one ate them. I do not know what will happen to the cannibals. Nobody wants them around.

The Indonesian guards beat the people and sexually assault the women. Officials take bribes for favorable treatment and to be put at the top of the list for relocation.

I am told that our camp has a high rate of resettlement, so I think my chances are good that I will see you someday. If I come to America, I want to go to college but I know I have to graduate from high school first. I am not too old to go back to school.

Almost everyone lives a boring life here waiting for resettlement. When someone is selected to be sent to another country the next step is to be transferred to Singapore to wait for two or three weeks to board an airplane for their new home. I pray for this day.

I have been assured that Vinh and I will not be separated. I have already started taking English classes so I can become a good American. That is my wish.

We only hope to have a good life like you someday. Thank you for any help you can give us.

Love,
Lien

CHAPTER 33

"Free to believe what I want."

The months, the weeks and even the days dragged on. Lien and Vinh fell into a routine. He went to school. She volunteered at the community garden, at the library, and swept the street and picked up litter on Saturday. On Sunday she took Vinh to the beach where he played in the water with the other boys and she tried to find a shady spot to sit and read a book. Lien attempted to read books printed in English because she thought it would prepare her to live in the United States. Her hours at the café were minimal and the administrators rarely called her to help in the office.

In the barracks Lien learned to live with little privacy. Under her watchful eye she kept fast maturing Vinh out of trouble. She stayed away from the guards and focused on blending in and not being recognized, which was not always possible because she was very pretty.

One hot afternoon she heard over the public address system, "Tran Thi Lien, Tran Thi Lien, come to the relocation office immediately. Tran Thi Lien, come to the relocation office immediately." Then the same message was repeated in Vietnamese.

She had not heard her full name spoken in so long she almost did not recognize it at first. Lien's pulse suddenly increased. Others in her barracks smiled at her and nodded; some wished her good luck. Being called to the relocation office could mean something very good or very bad.

She looked in the little mirror she had nailed to a wooden post and quickly brushed her hair, moistened her lips, and smoothed her blouse. She took a deep breath and squeezed her hands together in an attempt to keep them from trembling.

Walking rapidly, she breathed deeply. The office was close to her barracks. She quickly ascended the wooden steps to the open office.

It was a friendly face this time. "You are Tran Thi Lien?"

"Yes, sir. That is me."

"Please have a seat. Your English is quite good."

"Thank you, sir. My husband teach me."

"Well, I have good news for you," he said, renewing his smile. "Where does your husband live?"

"He live in Oregon, United States."

"But it says here on my papers that you are not married."

"Not yet, sir."

"OK. You'll have to figure that out for yourself. The Catholic Church will sponsor you and provide for your immediate needs in Salem, Oregon. They will provide you with housing, food, and take care of you and Vinh until you can stand on your own two feet."

"Oh, thank you, sir," and she began to cry. "I am so happy."

"We are happy to provide for this opportunity."

Then Lien stopped crying. "But what about my feet? My feet no problem. See, I can stand on two feet." And she stood.

The administrator said, "Stand on your two feet?" Then he laughed. "Oh no, 'stand on your own two feet' is an expression meaning being able to take care of yourself."

"I not know feet."

"It's OK. English is sometimes a funny language."

"Sir, I want to stand on my feet in America."

"And you shall."

This time they laughed together as she blotted the tears from her eyes.

"In three days," he said, "I want you and Vinh to come to this office with all your belongings packed. Be here at 10:00 a.m. You cannot bring more than you can carry. That means two bags each. We will take you and others in a van to the airport and you will fly to Singapore. It is a very short trip. Someone will meet you at the airport in Singapore and you will be processed for a passport to allow you into the United States. Then you will be taken to temporary housing."

"What you mean, tempry housing?" she asked.

"Temporary. It means short time housing. You won't be there very long. Maybe three weeks at the most. You will be provided food there. When your airplane comes it will take you to Portland, Oregon. Someone will meet you and others from Vietnam at that airport and take you to Salem, Oregon. What you decide to do from there is up to you. They will have English and citizenship classes for you and they will be able to make other arrangements for you. Do you have any questions?"

"I have *beaucoup* question, but don't know how to say," Lien said. "I be happy but afraid. That be OK?"

"That's only normal."

"I can't wait tell Vinh. He be happy too."

"It's a whole new life for both of you."

Lien sat there for a moment looking confused.

"Lien, don't worry. If you just do everything you are told, everything is taken care of. You don't have any personal choices to make until you get to Salem. The Catholic Church and the United States government want you. You are lucky. Some people nobody wants. If that happens, then they have to be sent back to Vietnam and they really aren't welcome there either."

"I go now?" Lien asked and stood.

"Yes, you can go now. And congratulations. Any country would be happy to have you."

She felt good about herself for the first time in a long time.

Three days later Lien and Vinh took a crowded van to a tiny airfield and boarded an old DC3 for the brief flight to Singapore. After they landed they were met by other vans to take them to a dilapidated two-story apartment building. For two weeks they had little to do except wait.

Lien found a couple paperback books someone had left behind and was delighted to see they were written in English. She struggled to read them.

One book was called Myra Breckinridge. It was about a man who had a sex change and pretended to be his dead wife until he was injured in a car crash. It had lots of sex but no love.

Another book was about the Peter Principle, which said that everyone who strives to improve their position in society or business will eventually reach their level of incompetence. They will be promoted beyond their ability. She was not quite sure she understood this but it made her think she had a long way to go on the social ladder. But in America, climbing that ladder was possible.

Both books were somewhat mysterious to her. She never knew, or even thought about, someone changing their sex. Lien had thought about improving her social and economic status, after all, that is why she became a Boat Person. But she never thought about someone advancing beyond their ability. *Maybe this is why so many leaders are failures*, she thought.

Both books represented a kind of freedom. *Maybe too much freedom in America was not a good thing. It seemed unnatural to allow someone to change their sex. And according to the Peter Principle everyone in a leadership position would be incompetent.* It was confusing, but she concluded that too much freedom was better than no freedom at all.

Then she got a radical idea. *I'm free to believe what I want. I don't even have to believe what I read. In America I can believe and say these writers are all wrong and no one can stop me.*

CHAPTER 34
Going to America!

<u>Singapore, 1977</u>

Early one morning most the refugees in the squalid Singapore Camp were told to line up at the administration building. Each family was called by name and led to the office. There, they were each given passports, a card documenting their inoculations, and handed a small amount of American currency. They were then told to pack all their belongings and stay in their rooms the next day.

This meant they were going to America! Lien was so excited she could not sleep that night. It was very hot all night. Lien fanned Vinh so he could sleep.

When her arm tired and Vinh had fallen asleep, she counted her new American currency. It was not a lot of money but it made her proud just to hold it. She thought about how all the American dollar bills were the same size and the same color. She would have to be careful to look at the numbers on the bills when she spent them. If she did not, someone might try to cheat her.

The next day, at noon, two young men came to their room and told them to bring their belongings to the front door of their tiny apartment. The men loaded their possessions onto vans waiting in the parking lot. The refugees were also told they could not bring food onto the plane, so they must leave it behind. What little they had was given to their neighbors who were not leaving yet. Once baggage and people were loaded, drivers drove them rapidly to the airport. With little time to survey their surroundings, they were hustled onto a huge shiny airplane.

Lien had never seen anything like it before. She had seen many helicopters, and had ridden in a cargo plane once, and observed fighters streak overhead, but never had she seen a plane so big it could have accommodated all of the people in the Lap Vo market.

Not only was it big, but clean and comfortable. The plane quickly filled with the refugees of war. They were told to put their luggage into the overhead bins. To the satisfaction of many, every seat was equipped with vomit bags. Some of the passengers were crying with emotion, some were praying, and some were smiling ear to ear. Lien was quiet and nervous. She did not want to celebrate or give thanks until the huge plane was in the air, over the ocean, and heading to America.

Before the plane taxied down the runway passengers were given flight safety instruction, which Lien did not fully understand but she knew enough to fasten her seatbelt.

Once in the air Vinh said he could not believe there was this much water in the world. He expressed that it was amazing to fly above the clouds. Whenever the plane bumped Lien saw her son grab the armrests. After an hour she fell asleep while Vinh kept staring out the window.

A couple hours later Lien woke briefly and found a blanket to cover herself. It felt very cold inside the airplane. Vinh wanted her to look out the window and she did, then smiled at him, and fell asleep again. She could not remember the last time she felt this safe. No fear of bullets or bombs, no fear of drowning or starving, and no fear of gangs and rape. As she slept she smiled and dreamed of America. She also dreamed of "Crint."

As evening approached, smartly dressed white women handed wrapped food on plastic trays. The food was bland and strange but filling. The peanutsand Coca-Cola, however, were a welcome treat.

When Lien woke again it was the middle of the night; she was surprised to see some other people awake too. Men were standing near the lavatory, smoking and talking quietly. A couple babies were making a fuss and their mothers were trying to calm them. A few people were standing in the aisles, alone with their thoughts.

When the plane began to descend, the stewardesses told people to take their seats and fasten their seatbelts. Lien was confused. Was the plane in trouble? Were they landing in Portland? Then she was told they were stopping in Japan to refuel. No one left the airplane and no one boarded. In a half hour they were in the air again and most people turned out the lights near their seat.

Lien wondered what Oregon would be like. She only knew what Clint had told her. It was green, had lots of trees, and cold compared to Vietnam.

She knew no relatives would meet her at the Portland airport like some of the passengers on the plane. She did not know any Vietnamese living in Oregon. In fact, she only knew one person in the entire state, and that was Clint, and he did not know she was coming.

Lien hoped Clint thought about her and the loving

household they once shared. Was he happy? Did he ever again feel such comfort and passion? Certainly, she had not. Lien remembered him the way he was and afraid he had changed. She wondered what he felt about their year together, if he marveled about their idyllic togetherness, or even if he thought about their life together at all.

When the communist took over most of South Vietnam, for her safety, they quit corresponding. They had not communicated since 1974. She wondered if he still loved her. *Since he was already married, maybe I am just a problem he would like to forget.*

She opened her floral cloth covered plastic purse. From inside the lining she recovered the last letter he had written her. In it was his address and phone number. She imagined Oregon was a big place, maybe bigger than Vietnam. Lien was not even sure she knew how to use a telephone to contact him. There would be a lot to learn in her new country, she realized.

Maybe Clint's American wife would kick him out of his house if his Vietnamese wife came knocking at his door. She smiled at the thought but realized she would not be brave enough to do such a thing. Besides, she did not want to hurt Clint even though she still resented him leaving her.

Lien began feeling nervous. This was supposed to be a happy flight but now she was feeling apprehensive. She wondered how she would survive in a new country alone, where she had difficulty with the language and had few skills. She thought that under communism everyone had their place, even if it was a bad place. In a country with freedom, she also had the freedom to fail. She may be hungry, homeless and unemployed in a strange, but free, new land. These thoughts worried her. She definitely would not be going back to sleep now, she thought.

The hours in the darkness passed as she looked out the tiny window next to her seat and saw nothing but the flashing lights on the wing of the airplane.

Her worry was interrupted by her memories of Clint. How they met in that horrible bar where she sold him beer and tea. How he paid to have sex with her the first time and how embarrassed she was. Her mother and father would have been ashamed of her. And how lucky she was that Clint turned out to be a kind person who took her away from the bar. When they made love in their own little house on the canal and later in their apartment in Can Tho, it was wonderful. When he left her each day she worried that he may not come back, but no matter how dirty and tired he was, he returned to greet her with a smile and a hug. Even though he may be grimy and sweaty, she welcomed his embrace. She heated water for his bath and she cooked him dinner. Then they made love on the sleeping pallet with a cloth covered foam rubber cushion.

When it was very hot day, they made love in their hammock. She laughed to herself, remembering the first time they tried the hammock together. They lost their balance; their legs became entangled in the netting, and were slowly dumped on the floor two feet below. So, that night they just made love on the rough wood floor and nobody got any splinters. They never got tired of being with each other, whether it was shopping, talking, or relaxing in each other's arms. She loved showing him the temples, the markets, and one time they went to a movie theater together.

He was so big and I was so small compared to him. But he was always gentle with me. I could have been afraid of somebody so strong, but I never was. Sometimes I was too jealous because he had a wife but that was not his fault. He was married before we met and he had a baby to take care of. I wish things could have been different and I am sorry that I criticized him for being married. It was not right for me to expect him to abandon his wife and baby.

I will always love him but if we meet again I will have to be strong and not make him feel guilty for taking care of his family. I will always be his Vietnamese wife even if we cannot get legally married.

Lien's eyes became heavy but she did not know if it was from wariness or from grief. A lump formed in her throat. For a moment she felt like she could not catch her breath. Even though she was elated to be going to America, the weight of unfulfilled love crushed down upon her.

She knew life could be so much better with Clint by her side. She also knew she must accept the possibility that this might never happen.

She needed to see him before she could know.

But she was also afraid to see him. Maybe the fantasy of him was better than the reality of him. She did not want to destroy that fantasy.

She could not live that fantasy not knowing the possibility of them being together again.

It was confusing. She wanted to think other thoughts. In the quiet of the airplane in the middle of the night over the ocean, feeling quite alone, other thoughts were not possible.

Every second that passed brought her closer to Clint. Whether it was closer just in distance, or emotion, she did not know.

CHAPTER 35

"Welcome to America"

The airplane trip seemed endless. And boring. Then Lien thought of the fishing-boat-trip-to-anywhere. It was horrifying. Boring was so much better than horrifying. And this time she knew the destination.

The destination was to a better life. It may not be a perfect life — she may never have Clint — but it was a life that she could make for herself. A young Vietnamese woman who befriended Americans and whose father was an officer who had fought with the French had no future in communist Vietnam. More importantly, her half American son had no future either.

Morning came early as they flew west toward the rising sun. People began to stir. The stewardesses got busy serving coffee.

Lien asked one of the flight attendants if she could help serve but she laughed at her. "Bless your heart. No sweetie. We can handle it. Y'all just relax now. What'd your boy like to drink?"

This English sounded different than what Clint tried to teach her. The accent was pretty, she thought. "He have milk with _café_," she said.

"And how would you like <u>your</u> coffee?" the stewardess asked.

"Hot."

The attendant smiled. "And black?"

"No, brown."

"Sugar?"

"Yes."

"How many lumps."

"One be OK," she guessed. Lien was surprised there were so many choices just for a cup of coffee.

After coffee and other drinks were served, packets of crackers and cookies were handed out. Lien was disappointed when she realized noodle soup would not be offered for breakfast.

Then the pilot came over the intercom. Lien strained to understand what he was saying. "Good morning ladies-n-gentlemen. It's my honor to welcome you and bring you to the United States. We stopped in Japan last night to refuel and are now 500 miles from the coast of the United States. We're flying at 32,000 feet, reducing altitude soon, and should see land in about an hour. We're making good time with the upper level winds helping us. In less than two hours we'll be landing at Portland International Airport. The temperature in Portland is 55 degrees with light rain. Visibility is 5 miles. The wind is calm, so we should have a nice soft landing. I understand there'll be people there to help you check in and to take you to your destinations in Oregon or Washington. Be sure to take all your belongings with you. Welcome to America."

Lien was not certain how far 500 miles was nor could she calculate 55 degrees but it sounded near and cold.

She looked at Vinh and said to him in Vietnamese, "Vinh, I want you to always remember this day. This is the most

GOODBYE VIETNAM

important day in your life. This is the beginning of our new life. Things will be better now."

"Yes, Mama," he said but without the enthusiasm Lien thought appropriate for the occasion.

"What do you want to be when you grow up?" She had asked him this many times in the past because his answer often changed.

Still waking and rubbing his eyes he said, "I want to fly an airplane like this one."

"In America you can learn to fly airplanes. You could never do that in Vietnam," she said.

When they landed Lien grabbed their bags from the overhead compartment. They all stood in the center aisle, unable to move. Someone came on board, gave a little talk which Lien could not hear, and guided everyone to a location in International Customs. Each was given one of five different colored name tags. Lien made sure Vinh had the same color as hers and stood next to him at all times. When processing was completed Lien and Vinh were guided to a waiting bus.

They sat down in the bus. Lien felt she and her son had been rushed through a confusing maize. Evidently they had done everything right because they were heading out of the big airport and was told by a guide they were traveling south toward Salem.

When they arrived at the Catholic Charities building it was another round of confusing paperwork. Lien did not try to understand, she just did whatever she was told. After Lien signed her name a half dozen times, she and Vinh were handed two pairs of sheets, two pillow cases, two pillows, given a room number and key, and pointed toward a dormitory. She was also told to meet in the main hall for breakfast and orientation the next morning.

Lien was pleased with the clean private room she would share with Vinh. They had separate beds and a bathroom equipped with a shower, sink and toilet. . Even towels and soap were provided. There was a common area outside her door where couches, magazines, and a television were available. Her first priority, however, was sleep.

The next morning, after bathing, they made their way to the cafeteria where a variety of American and Vietnamese food was available. The food was hot, abundant, and tasty.

By 9 a.m. orientation began and lasted throughout the morning. In the afternoon Lien met her counselor for the first time, signed-up for English class, and got Vinh registered in classes too. She looked at some of the job listings posted on the wall but knew she was not quite ready to join the job market.

In the afternoon she watched television and was amazed at the variety of programs. She began to realize there was much of the world she did not understand. It made her feel both challenged and unprepared.

On her third day she met with her counselor again. "I know someone in Oregon."

"That's wonderful."

"I like talk him. Can you help me?"

"Where does he live? Do you have his phone number?"

"I have." She pulled the envelope from her purse with his return address and his phone number she had written on the outside of the envelope.

"This is long distance. You can make only local calls."

"Can you call for me?"

"Is this someone who could give you a job?"

"Maybe. Maybe he give job."

"I'll call the number for you and see if I can get him. . . . It's ringing. . . . Hello, is Mr. McGregor there. This is Catholic Charities in Salem calling. . . . He is? . . . Can I get his number? . . . Yes, I've got it. Is this his office number? . . . OK, thank you very much. Goodbye."

"Lien, you did not tell me he's a state senator. I talked to his wife."

"I don't know state senator. He tell me he someday be senator."

"Well, that means he has an office in Salem and the legislature is in session now."

"Is that good?"

"Well, it means he is here in town and you can call him yourself. Do you know where the client telephones are?"

"It room next room with TV. I know where that."

"Can you dial the phone?"

"I watch you. I know."

"Well, here is the number. You don't have to dial the first three numbers since it is a local call." She handed Lien back her envelope where the counselor had written the local phone number.

"You show me what number to dial again?"

"Just these numbers," she said, and underlined the numbers for Lien.

"OK, I do." Lien smiled, stood and bowed to her.

"Lien, you don't have to bow to anyone in America. Everyone is equal. Good luck." The counselor smiled at her.

"Yes, ma'am," Lien said and quickly left the office.

Lien's heart fluttered as she made her way to the telephone room. She turned on the light. The little room was empty.

With trembling hands she dialed the number.

"Hello, Senator McGregor's office. How can we help you?"

"Hello, me want talk to Senator Crint."

"One moment please. Let me put you on hold for a minute."

Lien could hear the secretary. "Senator, I have someone on the phone who wants to talk to Senator Crint," she said with a mocking huff.

"To some people I'm Senator Clint. I'll take it in my office."

"She's on line one."

Lien heard a door shut.

"Hello, Senator Clint here."

"Crint, I miss you," Lien said as tears began to stream down her face.

"My God. Is this Lien?"

"Who else say Crint bad like me?" she said through laughter and tears.

"Where are you?"

"I here, Crint. I here Sarem. You here Sarem?"

"Yes, I'm in Salem. Where are you in Salem?

"I don't know, Crint. They take me and Vinh and other people on bus to Sarem. I need you find me. You want find me?"

"Of course I do. I have thought of you every day since I left Vietnam. How'd you get here?"

"I tell you. I come on bus."

"No, before that."

"It take me long time tell."

"I have the time."

"You come. You know Catholic Charity?"

"No. But I can find out."

"I don't know all rules. I have to make sure Vinh OK after school. I have to sleep here at night. You no sleep here."

"That's OK. We can go to dinner."

"I like. Can we kiss? That be OK?

"Just try to stop me."

"Crint, you still funny."

"Some people think I'm green behind the ears <u>and</u> funny."

"You no green. I see you everywhere. You smart. Someday I be smart too."

"OK. We are both smart, beautiful, and lonely and not green anywhere."

"Crint, you make me happy. You always say good thing."

"Lien, I can be there in about an hour. Will that be OK?"

"I wait for you."

CHAPTER 36
"I miss you."

Salem, Oregon, USA, 1977

At the reception desk Clint said, "Hello, I'm Senator McGregor. I'm here to see Tran Thi Lien."

The receptionist, an elderly woman volunteer, scanned a roster and said, "Can you say the name slowly and spell it for me? . . . Oh, here it is, I think . . . Tran Thi Lien (saying the middle name like 'thigh' instead of the correct 'tee')."

"Yes, that sounds like her name. Can I see her please?"

"Just sign here first and put the time." She turned the roster over to him and he signed where she pointed her finger.

"Just one moment," she said and walked to an office behind her carrying the sign-out sheet.

After a minute a man with graying hair and a white dress shirt with open collar came out. With a big smile on his angular face he extended his right hand. "Hi, I'm Glenn Samuels."

"And I'm Clint McGregor from the State Senate," he responded as they shook hands.

"You're Senator McGregor?"

"Yes, sir."

"And you're interested in seeing one of our residents?"

"That's right."

"I've been meaning to get over to the legislature. We have a bill in to help with our funding. I know helping Vietnamese

246

refugees may not seem like a state issue, but many of them will become state citizens and it's in all our interests to get them off to a good start."

"I agree. Perhaps we could meet in my office sometime to see how I can help. Here's my card. Call my secretary and see when we can meet. The best strategy would be to make this part of the state budget but we can talk more about that later."

"Thank you. I'll be happy to make an appointment."

"Afternoons are better for me but my secretary knows my schedule, so she'll set something up for us."

"Thank you. Now, you wanted to see . . ." and he picked up the roster where Clint had signed his name . . . "Tran Thi Lien? New resident."

"Yes."

"It's getting near dinner time and she has a son in school."

"I plan to take her to dinner and she said she would make arrangements for her son."

"We lock our outside doors at 10:00 . . . for security reason."

"That's understandable."

"I'll have someone go get her. She has not signed out."

With that he returned to his office and Clint sat in an uncomfortable wicker chair in the reception area. Although he had not been a senator very long, he had already become accustomed to everyone responding quickly to his requests. He sat impatiently.

After about 10 minutes Lien was guided to the reception desk and shown where to sign her name. Instead she ran to Clint, then restrained herself and bowed to him, "You must be Senator Crint," she said.

"Yes, I am," he said, suppressing a smile.

She turned and signed her name quickly. They passed through the front door, Lien in the lead and Clint following.

As soon as they reached a shady area in the parking lot she jumped toward Clint with both arms extended around his neck. As she wrapped her arms around his head he stood straight and lifted her off her feet.

She giggled. "Crint I miss you. Crint I miss you. I miss you."

He hugged her in return. "You are just as pretty as ever. I want your arms around me forever. I thought I would never see you again."

"Maybe God want us together. How you explain? How happen us?"

"I can't explain."

She kissed him. It was a long and searching kiss. "You make me *dien cai dau*."

Clint chuckled, knowing that term meant "crazy in the head." He looked around to see if they were being observed. "Come to my car," he said breathlessly. With one arm around her, he nearly carried her there. Opening the right front car door, he deposited her in the passengers' seat.

"Where we go?" she asked.

Once inside the car himself, he said, "Away from here. Let's go to The Ram. It's early; still warm. We can sit on the deck overlooking Mill Creek. Won't be many people there at this time."

"I know nothing. Take me anywhere, I go. But I cold. Be cold outside."

"We're going to have to go shopping. Buy you some

American clothes. But for now just grab my sweater in the back seat. It might look like a dress on you but it will keep you warm."

"Thank you, Crint. I do."

She struggled to put the big sweater on. She looked funny with big baggy sleeves and they both laughed.

"It smell like you. I like. I OK. I go Ram now," she announced.

When they entered the Ram, near the Capitol and Willamette University, Clint thought this was probably the perfect place to take someone who was unusually dressed. The clientele ranged from lobbyist with thousand dollar suits to college students with cut-off jeans and holey t-shirts. Someone wearing a huge sweater might not look out-of-place here.

The beautiful Vietnamese lady and the married state senator bumped knees and held hands underneath the table on the deck overlooking the babbling creek. They laughed and drank and as evening approached that sat close on the same side of the table and ate fish-and-chips and drank beer.

"GI, you buy me tea?" she joked.

"Hell, no!" he responded and kissed her.

They had a lot of catching-up to do. After a while Clint looked at his watch. "It's almost 9:30. I need to take you back," he said.

"Yes. Vinh be scared. He needs me."

"Yes, I understand." Clint paid the bill in cash and left a big tip. It was a wonderful evening.

They left the restaurant, Lien putting her arm around his. When they got into the car they kissed passionately, leaving them both aroused.

"You always good kisser," she said. "I feel heart me beat."

"The pleasure is all mine," he said.

As they drove back to Catholic Charities, Lien said, "Maybe we sleep together, like before."

"What about Vinh?"

"Not tonight."

"I hope sometime soon."

"Me too," she said.

When they arrived at the dormitories they embraced and kissed again in the car.

With an exaggerated motion she looked under the steering wheel and said, "I think you very happy see me."

"You made a joke."

"Maybe yoke, maybe no yoke."

"I'm happy we are together again."

"Toi yeu ban."

"I love you too."

Throughout the legislative session Clint and Lien spent as much time together as they could. On the weekends Clint made excuses to his wife why he could not spend time coming home. Vinh clung to Clint almost as much as Lien.

On the weekends Clint showed Vinh how to throw a baseball. They drove to Silver Falls State Park where they enjoyed picnics and hiked the trail that took them behind the waterfall. One weekend Clint rented a boat and cabin and they went fishing at Detroit Lake.

Lien continued to take English classes to learn how to speak and read "like an American."

"When I get good at English, I want to go to college," she said.

"What kind of classes would you take?" Clint asked skeptically.

"I like help people," she said. "Maybe I be counselor."

Clint had his doubts. "That sounds difficult. If you want to go to college you have to graduate from high school first, get good test scores, and then be sure to take something you can be successful at in college."

"You don't think me smart do you? You make me mad. Me no dumb peasant. You meet father me once. Did he sound dumb to you?"

"Actually, he didn't say much at all to me," Clint said.

"That because you don't know French. He know French but you don't speak it. I think he embarrassed you me live together."

Getting a little angry Clint said, "I'm sorry I did not meet his moral standards."

"No. It was me not meet his, what you say? Moral standard?"

Wanting to change the subject a little, Clint asked, "How are your parents?"

"Crint, how should I know? I can't call them on phone or write them letter.

Maybe they be punish because I run away from my country."

"Do you want to go back?"

"Crint, why you say wrong thing today, to hurt my feeling?"

"I'm sorry."

"They help me leave Vietnam even though it danger them. Maybe they be dead now and maybe I never know." Lien began to cry.

Clint put his arm around her. They sat on the couch in his Salem apartment and she put her head against his chest. He stroked her hair and wondered if she would leave him someday.

As she increased her knowledge of English and became comfortable with the culture, she gained more and more independence. He did not try to stifle her acculturation, even though it made their relationship more vulnerable.

When the legislative session ended, Clint had to return to Tillamook where he attended to his small real estate business, his children's activities, and community and political events. He saw less of Lien but included her in activities away from his district whenever he could. Nevertheless, her intense jealousy came to the forefront.

She wanted to be the only woman in his life. Clint volunteered to serve on every legislative interim committee in Salem so he could spend a night or two with her each week, but she demanded more of his time. He set her up with her own apartment and when she got a drivers' license he bought her a car, but still this was not enough.

Twice he attended conferences in Washington D.C. and took her with him. He introduced her to Blues Alley, the John F. Kennedy Memorial, and dinner in historic Fredericksburg, Virginia. But she refused to understand that he had to also attend some of the meetings while at a conference. She complained that during much of the day he left her and Vinh alone in their hotel room.

She complained. They discussed. He was frustrated. They loved each other but she wanted more of his time, while he felt that he was as generous with his time as possible. The love making was still good but he sometimes felt that it was the only comfortable part of the relationship.

"I give you and will continue to give you all of me that is possible to give," he said to her one night.

"Maybe that's not enough," she said.

He hugged her. She cried. And then they made love again. For a half-hour or so everything was perfect again.

With Clint's support Lien earned her GED, scored high on her SAT, and qualified for a college scholarship. In January 1979, she left Salem to enroll at Boston College. She said she was going to get a degree in social work.

And she did.

Although they corresponded the rest of their lives – first by mail and later by email – they saw each other infrequently. Always, they ended their correspondence with, "Love you." On holidays they talked on the phone. They made numerous plans to meet but their plans were often unfulfilled. The memories of each other were so precious they were afraid to lose them by seeing each other too often.

She never married. He was unhappily married.

Vinh became an airline pilot and often flew across the Pacific to Vietnam.

CHAPTER 37

"You Need a Counselor"

<u>Mountain Rest, South Carolina, USA, 2007</u>

Clint's phone rang. *Probably another telemarketer.* "Hello. I moved out in the sticks to get away from people like you."

"You want to get away from me, Crint?"

"Lien!"

"That's OK. Since we are good friends, you don't have to call me Ms. Tran." She giggled.

"Where are you calling from?"

"Boston, of course. Since you abandoned me I have not moved."

"I didn't abandon you. You up a left."

"Your history is muddled."

"How come you're still calling me Crint?"

"That's my name for you. Live with it."

"Like I have a choice," he said.

"I retired from the county. I've got a nice pension and a lot of freedom."

"I'm sure it's well deserved," he said. "I retired a couple years ago. It's a great life."

"Really? You still married to that woman?"

"She left me."

"She's smarter than I thought. Why'd she leave?"

"She said I'd rather read a book than talk to her."

"Was she right?"

"Yeah."

Lien giggled again. "Is that how you coped?"

"Well, I also drank a lot of beer," Clint admitted.

"You self-medicated for depression."

"Yes, that's a good way to put it."

"Are you fat now?" she asked.

"Just pleasantly plump. But strong. I could bench press you about 20 times."

"How interesting. Let me visualize that for a moment."

"What do you look like now?"

"I have a very nice personality."

"That's not what I asked."

"I know, but you need to grow up and realize that not everything is based on appearance. It's been a few years since we have seen each other. I guess now that you're retired you don't have anyone to pay for your conventions in Boston. I loved those Boston conferences. I learned so much. Oh, my looks? My hair is gray now, but sometimes that changes through the miracle of chemistry. To tell you the truth, I'm still slim and beautiful . . . for my age."

"I'd like to be the judge of that."

"I wouldn't mind. What is this place you're living at now? Mountain Rest: it sounds like where they put a bib around your neck, feed you with a spoon, and then give you a sedative."

"Are you serious? It's not like that all. I'm out in the boonies by myself with my dog, Lady, no supermarkets, no cable TV, no cleaning lady, no . . ."

"No female companionship?"

"None, whatsoever."

"How do you feel about that?"

"Now you're starting to sound like a counselor."

"I am a counselor, Senator Crint. How do you feel about that?

Clint paused for a moment. "I'm lonely, Lien."

"So am I Crint. I've been lonely for a long time."

"Why?"

"Now <u>you're</u> sounding like the counselor. You know, y'all startin' to git a Southern accent?"

"Are you changing the subject?"

"What subject?"

"Loneliness. We were talking about loneliness."

"Did I tell you I'm working on a new book?" Lien said.

"What's it about?"

"Codependency."

"Sounds like a best seller," he teased. "Is it about drugs?"

"Sort of."

"Let's get back to loneliness."

"If you wish. I've got the solution."

"To loneliness?"

"Yes."

"What is it?"

"Togetherness. You and me."

"I'm not moving to Boston. I like it here, where I chop my own firewood, hunt for my own food, and get my water out of the creek."

"And you're lonely."

"Well, yes."

"You need a counselor."

"You think so? Do you know a good one?"

"Yes. I'm coming to see you. And I'm bringing lots of luggage."

"How much is this counseling going to cost me?"

"We will work out a mutual services agreement."

"Are you sure? I live out in the woods."

"Remember, I grew up as a country girl."

"I remember."

"Remember when we had nothing together. No electricity, no running water, no bathtub . . ."

"I remember."

"Do you have an airport there?"

"Are you kidding?" he said. "You would have to fly into the Greenville, South Carolina airport. I could meet you there and we could drive to Mountain Rest."

"I'll make flight arrangements and call you back." Then she hung up.

Clint sat stunned. His life was about to change – for the better. He looked around his mountain cabin at the places that needed cleaning, the woodwork that needed repair, and the additional selves that needed to be built.

"Lady, come here."

She loped over to him. He hugged the big dog around the neck. "We are going to have to prepare for a visitor or a companion. I don't know which but I hope she's going to be our companion. You're going to like Lien. But first you need a bath."

The dog wagged her tail. Clint smiled.

Author's Note

Mixing real people, events, and places into a novel can be tricky. However, some of the events actually happened, may have happened, or could have happened. Every attempt has been made to portray the military mind-sent of the era accurately. The Vietnamese culture and attitudes are authentic as understood by an American observer and participant. Interestingly, some intelligence assumptions portrayed by this novel are being repeated in present day American foreign or military policy.

Three beautiful Asian women were an inspiration for this book: Tran Thi Ton, who will never read this book. Hoang-Nga Nguyen who saved me from some key writing blunders. And Sue Tse, my loving wife, who encourages me in every way.

Three writer critique groups, which I have participated in over the last few years, provided valuable advice when I needed it most: the Camden Chapter of the South Carolina Writers' Workshop; the Early Bird Critique Group of the Triangle Writers of North Carolina; and the Writers' Club of the Wynmoor Country Club of Coconut Creek, Florida.

Dell Isham
Happy Valley, Oregon
July 1, 2012

About the Author

Dell Isham was an Army officer and government advisor in South Vietnam in 1970 and 1971. He was awarded the Bronze Star for "meritorious service." His experience in the Mekong Delta provided him with the background to write this novel.

Prior to his military service he earned a B.S. degree in history from Weber State College (Ogden, Utah) and a M.A. degree in history from Colorado State University (Fort Collins, Colorado). After returning from Vietnam he taught at Siuslaw High School in Florence, Oregon, and was elected to the Oregon State Senate. He later was elected mayor of Lincoln City, Oregon, was appointed manager of the Devils Lake Water Improvement District, and was a lobbyist for 13 years. In 1997 he moved to South Carolina to be the Director of the South Carolina Chapter of the Sierra Club for 11 years.

Dell's previous books include <u>Rock Springs Massacre, 1885</u> and <u>Isom Dart and an Assortment of Scoundrels.</u>

He and his wife Susan live in Happy Valley, Oregon and Coconut Creek, Florida.

CPSIA information can be obtained at www.ICGtesting.com
Printed in the USA
BVOW08s0605271213

340191BV00001B/1/P